"Look, Would You Just Relax?"

"I don't get any more relaxed than this," she informed him.

"Sure you do. I've seen you."

Faith suddenly panicked. Cal wasn't going to refer to that New Year's Eve kiss, was he? Not after all this time.

"You know what you need? A back rub. And it so happens that I give the best damn back rubs on the face of this planet or any other. Guaranteed to get rid of the last bit of tension. It's worked on you before, remember?"

Faith remembered, all right. She'd been on the receiving end of his magical back rubs when they'd been in college. Ten years later she could still remember the languid pleasure. She didn't want a repeat performance.... Well, okay she might be tempted, but she was smart enough to recognize the road to disaster when she saw it.

Dear Reader,

Welcome to March and to Silhouette Desire! Our *Man of the Month, Wrangler's Lady,* is from an author many of you have told me is one of your favorites: Jackie Merritt. But this story isn't *just* a *Man of the Month,* it's also the first book in Jackie's exciting new series, THE SAXON BROTHERS.

Next: HAWK'S WAY *is back!* Joan Johnston continues her popular series with *The Cowboy Takes a Wife,* where we learn all about Faron Whitelaw's— from *The Cowboy and the Princess*—half brother, Carter Prescott.

The tie-ins and sequels just keep on coming, with Raye Morgan's *The Daddy Due Date*—a tie-in to last month's *Yesterday's Outlaw*—and BJ James's *The Hand of an Angel,* which continues her terrific books about the McLachlan brothers.

If you're looking for something completely different, you *must* pick up *Carolina on My Mind* by Anne Marie Winston. Here, our hero and heroine are abducted by aliens . . . and that's just for starters! And if you're looking for *humor,* don't miss *Midnight Ice* by Cathie Linz.

Miniseries and tie-ins, bold men and adventurous heroines, the supernatural and humor . . . there's something for *everyone* here at Silhouette Desire. So enjoy.

All the best,

Lucia Macro
Senior Editor

Please address questions and book requests to:
Reader Service
U.S.: P.O. Box 1325, Buffalo, NY 14269
Canadian: P.O. Box 1050, Niagara Falls, Ont. L2E 7G7

CATHIE LINZ
MIDNIGHT ICE

SILHOUETTE *Desire*®

Published by Silhouette Books

America's Publisher of Contemporary Romance

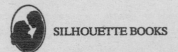

SILHOUETTE BOOKS

ISBN 0-373-05846-2

MIDNIGHT ICE

Printed in U.S.A.

Books by Cathie Linz

Silhouette Desire

Change of Heart #408
A Friend in Need #443
As Good as Gold #484
Adam's Way #519
Smiles #575
Handyman #616
Smooth Sailing #665
Flirting with Trouble #722
Male Ordered Bride #761
Escapades #804
Midnight Ice #846

CATHIE LINZ

was in her mid-twenties when she left her career in a university law library to become a full-time writer of contemporary romantic fiction. Since then, this best-selling Chicago author has had over twenty books published. In 1993 she won the *Romantic Times* Career Achievement Award for Best Storyteller of the Year. Cathie enjoys hearing from readers and has received fan mail from as far away as Nigeria!

An avid world traveler, Cathie often uses humorous mishaps from her own trips as inspiration for her stories. Such was the case with this book, inspired by a cruise to Alaska. Even so, Cathie is always glad to get back home to her two cats, her trusty word processor and her hidden cache of Oreo cookies!

To my niece Carrie, who grew up thinking her Auntie Cathie knew everything! Congratulations on getting that A in your honors English Lit class and on getting your Associate Degree. Good luck at Loyola!

One

"Look who's sleeping in my bed...."

At first, Faith Bishop thought that the raspy, full-of-the-devil baritone must be part of a dream. Then she heard it again.

"Wake up, Goldilocks."

Only one person she knew had that kind of outlaw voice. Her eyes flew open.

"You!" Faith blinked up at Cal Masters in dismay. "What are you doing here?"

"Sharing this cabin with you," Cal cheerfully replied. "Since you've laid claim to that bed, I guess I'll have to take this one." He strolled over and plopped himself down on the other twin bed a mere three feet away. "Ahh," he sighed. "That feels good. I didn't get much sleep last night."

No doubt he'd been frolicking with his latest hard-hearted girlfriend, Faith noted darkly before closing her eyes again in the hope that he'd disappear, that he was just part of some bad dream. No such luck. Opening her eyes again, she stared at him, unable to believe this was really happening to her.

Adventure, beautiful Alaskan scenery, gourmet food: these were the promises in the cruise brochures, and Faith had bought it all—along with a new wardrobe and a pair of contact lenses. This long-awaited vacation was supposed to be the trip of a lifetime. So far it had been more like a comedy of errors, which she was finding less and less amusing.

Absolutely nothing was going right. Last-minute problems at work meant that Faith had spent most of the previous evening scrambling to make a deadline instead of packing. Her job as senior editor for *Northwest Living* magazine had been particularly hectic these past few months with their being shorthanded by two positions. Attrition, management had called it. Chaos, Faith had privately called it . . . and lived it. She needed this vacation, badly!

She'd ended up getting only four hours' sleep last night. Consequently, upon her arrival in the cabin, she'd been unable to resist the temptation of resting for just a moment on the beckoning softness of the closest turned-down bed.

Although Faith had only been asleep a few minutes, her new contacts felt like sandpaper in her eyes. Which was, no doubt, why the manufacturer said to take out the contacts before going to bed, she reminded herself wryly. She doubted that her brief nap had helped her wild perm any, either. And now—to add insult to injury—instead of her girlfriend and cabin mate Chris, she had Cal Masters in the bed next to her.

At one time, ten years ago when they'd all been in college, Cal had been as close a friend to Faith as Chris was. Then, something had happened to change that. Wanting more than a platonic friendship, Faith had made a fool of herself over him. Neither she nor Cal had ever referred to the incident again, It was a moment Faith had never allowed herself to forget and it had affected her relationship with him ever since.

Not that Cal had been around a lot. He'd spent seven of the last ten years as a journalist for a weekly national newsmagazine, covering the world's hot spots. During that time, Faith certainly hadn't been pining away for him. She'd gotten on with her life, a life she found very satisfying.

"Listen, Cal, I'm not in the mood for practical jokes here. So get off that bed and tell me what's going on," she stated while hurriedly getting up from the twin bed on which she'd been resting.

In keeping with the kind of day it had been so far, she ended up tipping over her suitcase and knocking her open maroon tote bag to the floor in the process. Its contents were now strewn all over the carpet. Giving Cal an impatient look, she said, "Look what you made me do!"

"I'm looking," Cal assured her, leaning over to pick up a slinky leopard-print item and hold it up to the light. "Nice nightie. Follows the philosophy that less is more. I like that. I definitely approve."

"That is not mine!" Faith haughtily informed him, angry with herself for noticing the artistic leanness of Cal's hands as he held the little bit of nothing in his hands.

"Well, it's certainly not mine," Cal mockingly countered.

Faith was only now realizing that nothing that had fallen out of the tote bag looked the least bit familiar to her. "None of this is mine," she noted in dismay.

"Pity," Cal stated. "I was looking forward to seeing you in this little...*very* little number." He swirled the scanty, see-through nightie around his index finger.

"Give that back." She grabbed it from him and in doing so, her fingers brushed against his. The contact was electrifying And somewhat terrifying—for her. She doubted Cal even noticed the brief touch. But it was enough to almost send her into a panic.

Calm down. You can handle this, she reassured herself, stuffing the nightie back into the tote bag along with the other things she'd hurriedly picked up. She tried to ignore the slight tremble of her fingers and instead focused on the unfamiliar items around her. "Obviously this stuff belongs to someone else." She frowned at a skimpy red satin kimono with a black dragon emblazoned on it. "I must have been given the wrong bag by mistake. It looks just like my tote bag on the outside . . . same size, make and color. But these are *not* my things."

"Too bad," Cal drawled. "I thought maybe you'd turned over a new leaf in your old age."

Faith *had* turned over a new leaf. Or was trying to. Hence the contacts, which Cal hadn't so much as mentioned. Not that she really expected him to. He'd never noticed anything about her in the past, why would he start now at this late date?

She, meanwhile, continued to notice entirely too much about him. Cal never seemed to change, unless it was to get even sexier as he got older. His slow smile still had that desperado edge to it. She'd always attributed it to the fact that he liked watching Westerns, Clint Eastwood's spaghetti Westerns in particular. In their college days, she and Cal had spent more than one evening watching *The Good, The Bad and The Ugly* together, being the only two Western-movie aficionados in their coed dorm.

In those days, his brown hair had always looked slightly tousled. It still did. It was a look that some men spent hours trying to attain in a trendy hair salon. Not Cal. That's just the way his hair was.

His smoky blue eyes, with their slight downward slope at the outer edges, had always had the power to make Faith's heart beat faster—from the very first time she'd seen him across a study table in the library her freshman year in college. *She'd* melted. *He'd* looked past her to the blonde standing behind her. And so it had always been.

She knew that. She wasn't a starry-eyed romantic twenty-one year old any longer. Those times were long gone. She, like Cal, was now in her early thirties. Unlike Cal, she'd even been married once—briefly, right after she'd graduated from college. She'd married a teaching assistant who ended up spending most of his time on archaeological digs in Mexico. The marriage had only lasted a year.

So here she was, a divorced woman who was having a bad hair day. And to top things off, her contacts were blurring her vision. Not blurring it enough, however, that she still couldn't see how great Cal looked in jeans and a red shirt.

And what, Faith wondered, did Cal see when he looked at her? Her honey-colored hair waved into the-perm-from-hell? Her eyes, that couldn't make up their mind whether to be brown or green? The five pounds she'd hoped to lose before coming on this trip, but that still prevented her from getting into a size twelve?

Cal had once told her that she had a "cute" face. At the time, Faith had hoped it meant he thought she was pretty. Now she knew it simply meant she wasn't beautiful. Instead, she was "cute."

She glared at Cal as if it were his fault that she was having these self-doubts about her attractiveness. Over the years, she'd come to terms with her looks. She might not be a raving beauty, but then she wasn't a complete slouch in that department, either. There were things that she *did* like about her looks. Plenty of things.

Her nose, for one. A French major in college had told her it was *retroussé*.

Her lips were another positive. They were bow-shaped, or so she'd been told by the photographer who'd taken her Christmas picture for her parents. The guy had raved on and on about her lips, *delectable* was the term he'd used.

But delectable though her lips were purported to be, they had only felt Cal's lips upon them once in her life—and the experience had ended in her utter humiliation.

"Where are you going?" Cal demanded as she headed toward the door of the cabin.

"To find a purser and straighten this luggage problem out," Faith replied. "While he's at it, maybe he can direct you to your cabin, if you really are sailing on this cruise."

"I already know where my cabin is," Cal replied. "I'm in it."

"Don't be ridiculous. Chris and I are sharing this cabin," Faith told him. "She's flying in from Seattle to join me here. I drove up to Vancouver from Seattle and left my car there for our return trip. The cruise ends in Vancouver, you know."

"I know," Cal said.

"Anyway, I left my car in Vancouver and flew up to Anchorage, but the flight was late, so I was rushed onto a bus and convinced to part with my tote bag even though I didn't think it was a good idea at the time." Faith knew she was babbling but she didn't care. Cal made her nervous. And talking made her feel better. "We get here to Whittier where the boat was waiting—"

"Ship," Cal inserted with masculine impatience. "Not boat."

"Chris is meeting me here," Faith firmly stated, repeating the sentence as if it were a talisman guaranteed to ward off evil spirits. "We're sharing this cabin."

"You and Chris *were* sharing this cabin," Cal corrected her. "But that was before she broke her leg last night. Her cast is as big as a house. I know, I saw her right before I left. Needless to say, she won't be accompanying you on this trip. I will."

"What do you mean?" Faith asked, even though she had a sinking feeling she already knew darn well what he meant.

"Chris didn't take out travel insurance, so she would have lost all the money she'd paid for the cruise if I hadn't helped her out. I had some free time, I've never been to Alaska before and I've been meaning to take a trip up here. So I bought Chris's ticket from her and I'm taking her place."

"You can't do that."

"Too late. I already have," Cal said, settling in on the bed and making himself even more comfortable by clasping his hands behind his head. "Why the shocked look, Faith? It's not as if we don't know each other."

Everything Faith knew about Cal made her want to run in the opposite direction. And the things she knew about *herself*—specifically, that damn crush she'd had on him—weren't very reassuring, either.

Against her will, more memories came rushing back. From the first moment Faith had seen Cal in the library, her breath had caught in her throat and her heart had leapt up to keep it company. Unfortunately, it had quickly become apparent to her that while Cal made her blood flow faster, she'd had zip effect on him. That hadn't stopped her quiet crush from growing, however.

Things had come to a head at a New Year's party her senior year in college. Deciding it was now or never, Faith had taken her faltering courage in hand. When everyone was celebrating the early arrival of the new year at Times Square on the other end of the country, Faith had walked straight up to Cal and kissed him.

Even now, Faith could feel a blush heating her cheeks as she recalled with devastating clarity what had happened next. Cal had pushed her away and then he'd gone on to kiss someone else—a gorgeous blonde with a perfect face and perfect hair.

By the time midnight had finally arrived in Seattle's Pacific time zone, Faith was alone in her dorm room—crying her eyes out. She'd vowed it would be the last time she'd allow herself to cry because of Cal.

It was a vow she'd kept until six months ago, when Cal had collapsed at Seattle's airport with a near deadly case of double pneumonia he'd picked up while covering the strife in war-torn Bosnia. As he'd lain there in a hospital bed, unconscious and as pale as the white sheets covering him, she'd taken his hand in hers and quietly wept.

Cal, being Cal, had chosen that moment to regain consciousness. "You're getting me all wet," he'd croaked mockingly.

Wiping her tears away, she'd looked into his smoky blue eyes and known.... Known she was still vulnerable to his brand of charm. It had been a heartrending discovery.

Along with relief at knowing he'd be all right, Faith realized then and there that she'd have to protect herself as best she could from further exposure to his potent charm. So throughout the past few months, Faith had carefully kept her distance from Cal.

But how the heck was she supposed to keep her distance from him in a cabin the size of a postage stamp? Looking at him sprawled out on the twin bed a few feet away from her, Faith saw the potential for great trouble here. Major trouble.

She needed to get away from him. She needed some time to clear her thoughts. She needed to find her damn tote bag!

After hastily grabbing the tote bag and opening the cabin door, Faith was lucky enough to spot a purser a few feet down the hallway. "Excuse me, but I need some help."

"Certainly, ma'am. How can I be of assistance?" the purser asked as he joined her outside her open cabin door.

"There seems to be a problem with my luggage," Faith told him. "The bag I've got isn't mine." She handed it over to him. "It's the same kind of bag as mine, same size, make and color, but it isn't mine."

"I'm so sorry, ma'am. I'll get on it right away."

"Listen, while you're at it, could you check and see if there are any other outside cabins available on this level?"

"You and the gentleman wish to move?" the purser asked, apparently having spotted Cal through the open door.

"No, I wish to move. The gentleman can stay where he is," Faith said with a glare over her shoulder at Cal, who was still lounging on the bed. He had the nerve to actually wave at her.

"I'm sorry, but there are no openings on this level, ma'am," the purser said. "Inside or outside. We may have a few openings on the upper deck, but you'd have to pay the additional charge."

Stepping away from the door to get a little privacy, Faith asked the purser how much the additional charge would be. When he told her, Faith gulped before saying, "Never mind. We'll stay where we are. Thank you."

"As you wish, ma'am. Meanwhile, I'll try to locate your tote bag for you. I'm sorry you've had this trouble."

"I'm sorry, too," Faith muttered. Sorry about Chris's accident and broken leg. Sorry the purser kept calling Faith ma'am as if she were eighty. Sorry she couldn't get rid of Cal. Sorry she couldn't afford the luxury of upgrading to a cabin of her own. But she'd saved all year for this cruise as it was. There was no way she could afford to go further into hock.

She would just have to make the best of a sticky situation and not allow Cal's unexpected presence to ruin her trip for her. She wouldn't let him. It was that simple, and Faith vowed to keep it that way.

"Missing? How can bag be missing?" Ivan Yurilov demanded of his cohort Natasha in their inside cabin. A short man who reminded Agatha Christie aficionados of Hercule Poirot without the brains, Ivan worriedly rubbed his dark mustache.

"Quiet!" Natasha Bustov snapped. She towered over him by at least four inches. Her parents had both been Silver Medal shot-putters in the Olympics. She'd inherited their height but not their bulk. "You want everyone should hear you? Speak English," she added as Ivan lapsed into their mother tongue.

"You told me bag would be safe," Ivan said.

"I only set down bag for second. They took it. Could not get back. Told me would be fine. Bag will be in room."

"Bag is not in room," Ivan countered. "This bag—" he held it up for her to see "—is not ours."

"I know is not ours."

"You know where our bag is?"

"No. But we will find."

"We better find," Ivan said ominously. "Valuables can not go missing."

"Valuables will not go missing," Natasha assured him, swishing her nearly waist-length black hair over her shoulder before frowning. "You do not think it is curse, do you?"

"Do not speak of curse to me," Ivan flared. "Is not true. Valuables are not cursed. *We* are not cursed."

Natasha nodded. "You are correct. We must not overreact. Peoples will get suspicious. Must act calm."

"Calm?" Ivan repeated. "How can I be calm after what we lived through? Who would think there would be coup on Nabassi Island after all these years? Who would think we would end up with such...valuables?"

"Who would think our government would collapse and we would be out of job?" Natasha retorted.

"Thirty years I devoted to mother country. I give best years of my life to serve Communist party! What do I get? Fired!"

"Is best we look out for ourselves," Natasha declared.

"To do that, we need valuables," Ivan reminded her.

"Of all the cruise ships in all the oceans in the world, you gotta walk onto mine," Cal drawled as Faith rejoined him in their cabin. He was still lounging on the bed, propped up against a pile of pillows like a sultan waiting for his harem.

"I was here first," she retorted. "By rights, that line should be mine."

"You don't have the voice for Humphrey Bogart impersonations," he countered.

And she didn't have the slinky figure or husky voice for Lauren Bacall impersonations, either, she reminded herself. With this curly perm, she felt more like Shirley Temple.

"Since we're going to be sharing this small space for the next week, I've written up a list of rules to make living together easier," Cal declared.

Faith took the notebook he handed her, taking care that her fingers didn't touch his. She didn't want any more sensual electricity shooting through her nervous system today, thank you very much. She was fast reaching the end of her tether.

Given his journalism background, she knew that Cal was never without a notebook, but she didn't know he was so gung ho on rules. He never used to be. And then she began reading them.

"No parading around naked unless it's by request!" she repeated in disbelief.

"That a problem for you?" he inquired with wicked innocence. "If so, I suppose I could relent on that one."

"Very funny, Masters." Calling him by his last name helped to distance herself. It was either that or strangle him. "What's this? No bras, undies or stockings hanging from the shower rail?"

"Hey, I gotta draw the line somewhere," he maintained.

"You know what you can do with your outrageous rules, don't you?"

"The look on your face gives me a pretty good idea," Cal replied.

"Good." She took his pen from the nightstand and crossed off his ridiculous rules, replacing them with practical ones of her own before handing the notebook back to him, so angry that she actually shoved it at him.

"What's this?" he said. "A midnight curfew? Faith, Faith..." He shook his head admonishingly. "I haven't had a curfew since I was sixteen, and even then I didn't pay much attention to it."

"We're on this cruise to see the scenery," she reminded him.

"Speak for yourself," Cal retorted.

"If you wanted a ship filled with the blond bimbos clad in skimpy bikinis, you should have taken a cruise to the Caribbean," Faith snapped, irritated by his attitude.

"I wasn't given that option," he returned.

"Early to bed, early to rise, makes a man..."

"A pain in the butt," Cal inserted.

"Why are you going out of your way to make this difficult?"

"I'm not going out of my way. I just think you should loosen up a little. We're sharing a cabin, not the rest of our lives. It's not the end of the world."

That's what you think, Faith silently noted. It might not be a big deal to him, but it was to her—determined though she was not to show it. Clearly it was time for another approach. "Fine. Let's just have one rule then. That we keep out of each other's way."

"Sounds good to me," Cal agreed.

"Great." It was only now occurring to Faith that it was a mistake for her to be afraid of the seductive magic of Cal's touch. That only gave him more power over her. The thing to do was to make herself immune to him and his damn magic. "We'll shake on it then." Faith held out her hand, pleased to see it didn't tremble at all. Anger did a lot to steady one's nerves.

Faith reassured herself by likening this new treatment to that of using snake venom as an antidote to a snakebite. Deliberately touching Cal in a no-nonsense way was part of her recovery. She wanted, no... she *needed* to prove something to herself here. That the earlier jolt of awareness had been a fluke. That she was over him. Or at least well on the road to complete recovery.

Faith braced herself as Cal shook her hand. This time no fireworks exploded. The ground beneath her feet, which had a tendency to shift up and down with the swell of the waves, anyway, didn't move any more than it had since she'd first boarded the cruise ship. Nothing earth-shattering occurred. Instead, a small corner of her heart quietly tucked the memory of his hand surrounding hers into its memento book. A harmless enough occurrence, surely?

Faith quickly tugged her hand away. The bottom line was that she'd survived it. And she would survive the next week, as well. She'd even have a good time doing so. All she needed was her missing tote bag and she'd be ready to face anything—Cal Masters included.

Two

—

"Isn't this nice and cozy?" Cal said as he watched Faith unpack the suitcase she *did* have. He knew he shouldn't tease her so, but she always took the bait so beautifully. For all her quiet ways, Faith never failed to make him feel alive.

She'd done something to her hair. The wild waves made her face seem even more delicate. Her creamy white skin allowed him to see her every blush. And he used to make her blush a lot when they were in college—without even trying.

He couldn't remember their first meeting. In some ways, it seemed as if she'd just always been there. They'd had some great times together in the old days. He definitely remembered those. He even remembered the little things like sharing salami and artichoke heart pizzas while everyone else, unappreciative gourmands that they were, made gagging noises; sleepless nights during exam week spent playing no-holds-barred games of Ping-Pong downstairs at three a.m. while reciting the names of the pharaohs of Egypt for Western Civ 101; her reading his stories and suggesting ways to tighten them up. Just Faith and him. She'd always been just Faith. He hoped she still was.

Which was why he'd teased her so mercilessly. She'd been distancing herself from him during the past year. Since his illness six months ago, to be exact. She probably thought he was a puny idiot. He'd made a joke of it at the time, something about it being unheroic of him to collapse because of a damn virus when gunshot wounds were so much more romantic. He'd wanted to make her smile. Instead, he'd made her angry.

Which was okay with him. Anything to stop her crying. He was no good with tears.

He was also no good with long recuperations like the one necessary for him to completely recover. As Faith had mockingly accused him at the time, he hadn't been content to just have pneumonia, he'd had to get double pneumonia. An atypical one. Mycoplasma pneumonia. And then he'd had to go and get nonrespiratory complications. The doctors had told Cal that relapse was a feature of the disease and he hadn't proved them wrong. Myalgia, nausea and a host of Latin terms meaning he felt as weak as a baby and about as steady on his pins.

The magazine had grounded him, forcing him to take a six-month leave of absence. After six weeks, he'd been ready to climb the walls when he'd gotten the surprising temporary job offer from one of Seattle's more experimental colleges. Teaching a special journalism course for a quarter hadn't been one of Cal's career goals, but he had to admit he'd enjoyed stirring things up. It was a specialty of his. He liked to think the students who'd taken his course were the better for it. And he'd certainly enjoyed rattling a few academic cages while he was at it.

To Cal's surprise, the college had offered him a position teaching full-time next year. He hadn't given them an answer yet. The summers off would give him time to work on that adventure novel he'd been wanting to write. But he wasn't eager to give up his job with the magazine and the freedom that it entailed. Still, he was considering the college's offer....

Funny how almost dying changed your perspective on things. Turned them upside down. The truth was, Cal didn't know what he wanted. He still had three weeks left on his leave of absence, and for now all he cared about was kicking back and having a little fun.

"Yeah, this is nice," Cal repeated with a slow smile in Faith's direction. "A real domestic scene."

"Oh, it's just peachy," she retorted. After their handshake, she'd slipped into the bathroom to remove her scratchy contact lenses and put her glasses back on. The black frames gave her a studious look that went well with her position as editor, but didn't fit the look she'd been trying to achieve on this cruise.

Feeling self-conscious, Faith impatiently pushed her slipping glasses back into place on the bridge of her nose and glanced at Cal in exasperation. "You really don't have to sit there and watch my every move, you know. You could go up on deck and look around."

"I could," Cal agreed. "But I don't want to."

"God forbid you should do something you don't want to," Faith muttered under her breath. Being the center of his attention was disconcerting, to put it mildly. She needed to distract him, so she asked, "Where is *your* luggage?"

"Over there." Cal pointed to a battered backpack she hadn't noticed in the corner.

"Where's the rest of it?"

"That's all there is. I travel light," he murmured with one of his knock'em-dead grins.

"Good," she said briskly. "Then you won't need much closet space. There isn't much room in here," she noted, looking inside the built-in cabinet that housed the closet as well as a chest of drawers. Backing up, she almost ran into Cal. "*Now* what are you doing?"

"Checking out the closet space," he replied, looking over her shoulder. "Thought I might as well unpack now, too."

Faith decided she'd made a tactical error by asking him about his luggage. Her heart was pounding to beat the band as a result of his nearness. She'd definitely felt safer when he was on the bed rather than on the loose, prowling around the tiny cabin.

"There isn't room in this cabin for both of us to unpack at the same time," Faith stated.

"There's plenty of room," Cal countered.

Cal loved contradicting her, Faith recalled irritably. He always had. One of his less endearing traits.

He was close enough to be her shadow. It seemed she couldn't turn around without brushing against him as he removed his folded shirts and jeans from his backpack. The clothing she saw him putting away did not reassure her, as the matter of his sleeping attire suddenly came to mind. "Uh, that is, um . . . you did bring a pair of pajamas with you, didn't you?" Faith inquired with attempted nonchalance.

"Yep. Brand-new pair. Still in the package."

She heaved a silent sigh of relief. "Good."

"Of course, I'm only going to be wearing the bottom half. You're welcome to use the top half if you'd like," he offered her with mock generosity.

"No, thanks," Faith coolly replied, wishing she could have thought of something equally mocking to say instead of sounding as if she'd just gotten out of a convent. "I've got pajamas of my own."

"Satin ones." At her startled look, Cal added, "I saw you put them away."

While aware of his attention, Faith hadn't realized he'd been watching her *that* closely. It made her glad she'd camouflaged her pile of silky underwear in a T-shirt as she'd stuffed them all into a drawer.

"This drawer taken?" Cal asked, tugging out the top one before she could answer. There was her underwear, in colorful disarray. He raised an eyebrow at the silky bits of nothing. He'd have expected her to wear sensible cotton.

"Yes, that drawer is taken," Faith exclaimed, slamming the drawer closed so fast Cal narrowly missed getting his fingers squashed.

"I *have* seen a woman's underwear before, Faith," Cal solemnly assured her.

"I'm sure you have." But not *mine,* she silently added, not appreciating the speculative look he'd given her—as if she were the last woman on earth he'd have expected to wear slinky underwear.

Seeing the way her chin lifted a notch or two, Cal sighed, recognizing the surefire signs of Faith about to step into battle. "Look, would you just relax?"

Sensing that he was about to put his hands on her shoulders, Faith did a quick sidestep that took her out of his reach, or as far as she could get in their cramped quarters. "I don't get any more relaxed than this," she informed him.

"Sure you do," he contradicted her yet again. "I've seen you."

Oh, God, Faith silently panicked. He wasn't going to refer to that New Year's Eve kiss, was he? Not after all this time.

"You know what you need?" he asked.

"Some peace and quiet," Faith immediately replied.

"No. A back rub. And it so happens that I give the best damn back rubs on the face of this planet or any other. Guaranteed to relax the toughest customer. Magic fingers." He held them up and wiggled all ten digits at her teasingly. "These are my secret weapons. Guaranteed to get rid of the last bit of tension. It's worked on you before, remember?"

Faith remembered, all right. She'd been on the receiving end of his magical back rubs when they'd been in college. Ten years later she could still remember the languid pleasure she'd felt. She didn't want a repeat performance.... Well, okay, she might be tempted, but she was smart enough to recognize the road to disaster when she saw it.

She looked up to politely refuse his offer, but the words got stuck in her throat as she fell prey to the alluring intensity of his wicked blue eyes. In the few times she'd seen him since his illness, she'd tried to make it a practice not to look directly into his eyes for very long. She suspected that if she did, she'd turn back into the tongue-tied wallflower she'd been in college.

The rest of the time, she was confident in her abilities. She knew she had a good head on her shoulders, that she was a damn fine editor. She had awards and degrees on her office wall to support the fact that she excelled at what she did.

But now, as she got caught up in the magic of Cal's eyes, reality went haywire. Held spellbound in that moment, it was easy for Faith to believe that Cal actually had the power to steal her soul and her heart right out of her—and that there wouldn't be a damn thing she could do about it.

The knock on the door shattered the sudden silence as surely as a hammer shatters glass. That quickly, the spell was broken and Faith regained her equilibrium. Reality returned. Welcoming the interruption, she hurried to the door and opened it.

The purser was standing there. "Miss Bishop, I believe we found your tote bag for you," he said. "It doesn't have a name tag on it, however," he added disapprovingly.

Faith flushed, telling herself her reaction was a result of the purser's implied criticism and not the disturbing moment she'd just shared with Cal. "The bag is new and I ran out of time last night when I was packing. I didn't plan on having the bag stowed with the rest of the luggage.... I told your representative that when they took it away. They marked something on their chart, a description of the bag, I'm assuming..."

"Yes, well, if you'd just check to make sure this is indeed your bag..." the purser inserted, handing it to her.

Faith unzipped the tote bag and saw her makeup case, which she'd packed on the top. "It's mine." Just to be sure, she looked further and saw her pillow with its purple floral design pillowcase. "Definitely mine."

"Good. We apologize for the mix-up," the purser said before making his departure.

"Everything back to normal now?" Cal inquired as he watched Faith carry her tote bag over to her twin bed as if it were a huge stuffed toy prize she'd just won at a carnival.

As normal as they could be, Faith thought to herself, given the fact that she would have to spend the night—and the next six nights—in a very small cabin with a man who had once held the key to her heart.

"I am going to use American phrase here," Natasha said. "We have good news and bad news, Ivan. Good news is we have bag back. Bad news is valuables are missing."

"Missing?"

Natasha nodded.

"Not in bag?" Ivan asked.

"Not in bag," Natasha confirmed.

"I told you was stupid idea to hide valuables in face-cream jar."

"Was not stupid idea," Natasha protested. "Was brilliant idea. No one looks in jar for diamonds. Not when jar is full of face cream."

"Someone did look," Ivan stated. "Someone stole!"

"*We* stole," Natasha agreed. "And curse says stones of Midnight Ice will bring darkness to all who hold them," she reminded him with a meaningful look.

Ivan waved her words away. "Curse is foolish! Is not true. I told you not to mention again! We have other problems. Someone stole from *us*. I told you America is full of thieves," Ivan stated dramatically. "Now peoples, thieves, have stolen from us! Stole valuables worth hundred thousand dollars or more. Diamonds are pension plan for us. For our old age. Communist party will no longer take care of us. Is best we take care of ourselves."

"Only if we find diamonds can we take care of ourselves," Natasha said.

"We will find," Ivan replied. "*You* lost bag. *You* find diamonds."

"Is not my fault," Natasha declared, drawing herself up to her full height and towering over Ivan.

Ivan hurriedly stepped back a step or two. "No time to argue now."

"I did not loose diamonds." Natasha frowned at the sound of that. Something sounded wrong to her. "Correction. I did not *lose* diamonds. Was not my fault. I was not one banished to Nabassi Island because of incompetence," she reminded Ivan with a glare.

"Was not incompetence," Ivan denied. "Was jealousy. I was smarter than my superiors and they did not appreciate fact."

"They did not appreciate fact that you had reputation of being called Ivan the Impossible... because was impossible for you to do job correctly!"

"Do not forget, *you* had same reputation," Ivan angrily reminded her. "You were sent to Nabassi Island for same reasons. Failures. I was one who trained you when you first came to island. I was one who let you read secret procedure manual to train you to be spy someday. Do not forget who gave you chance," Ivan said with an angry shake of his finger. "Who brought you with when I left Nabassi?" he demanded. "Me." Ivan smacked his chest. "Who saw chance for better life? Me." Another openhanded smack to his chest. "Who thought of master plan?"

"Me," inserted Natasha, proudly throwing back her shoulders and displaying her own impressive chestline.

"Okay, you thought of master plan," Ivan acknowledged, "but I did many things too. Do not forget that."

"I do not forget. We are partners now, Ivan."

"Partners who have no valuables," Ivan glumly reminded her.

"We will find diamonds. Because no one steals from Natasha Bustov!"

* * *

"Yoo-hoo, Calvin!"

"Oh, no," Cal muttered as he and Faith entered the ship's dining room for dinner, which had open seating this first evening.

"Yoo-hoo! Over here, Calvin!" The shrill voice was accompanied by enough waving to do a cheerleader proud.

"Ignore her, maybe she'll go away," Cal ordered Faith.

"Who is she?" Faith asked.

"Some woman I met on the bus from Anchorage," Cal replied. He recalled how the woman had gotten completely flustered when their bus had pulled onto a train to ride piggyback on a flatcar through the tunnel leading to Whittier, the railroad line being the only access to the port town. "I can't tell if we're coming or going," she'd exclaimed. "No," her female traveling companion had inexplicably replied, prompting Cal to dub the two "The Twilight Twins."

"She's not going to let you ignore her," Faith warned him. "She's coming this way."

"We saved you a seat, Calvin," the woman announced, grabbing him by the arm and trying to tug him after her. Since he didn't move, she bounced back like a bungee cord. She tried again, pulling a little harder this time. "Come along, dear."

"Thanks but—"

"We'd be glad to join you," Faith interjected, only to receive a glare from Cal.

"Who are you?" the woman demanded.

"A friend of Calvin's," Faith replied with a grin.

"My name is Cal," he declared between clenched teeth. "Not Calvin."

"Whatever you say, Calvin." The woman patted his arm, and tugged on it again. "Come along now."

"Yes, Calvin. Do come along," Faith seconded sweetly, delighted to see him discomfited since it was such a rare occurrence.

The look Cal gave her warned her that he was going to make her pay for this, but Faith didn't care. For the first time since she'd woken up to find him hovering over her, she felt as if she had the upper hand for a change. For the past two hours, Cal had taken great delight in aggravating her. Now it was payback time.

The sight of the petite older woman dragging Cal after her toward a table for six as if he were a trophy made Faith's smile widen. She followed along at a more leisurely pace, surprised and delighted at the appreciative looks she was getting from one of the uniformed officers at the captain's table. Since this first night's dinner on the ship was rather informal, she'd elected to wear black slacks and a flowing poet's shirt in pale apricot—both in rich washable silk. With *this* outfit, her glasses looked stylish rather than studious.

"Here he is," the older woman declared proudly. "You remember my friend Rhoda, don't you, Calvin?"

Cal nodded at the second, and infinitely more silent, member of the Twilight Twin twosome.

"And over there are the Kecks—Bud and Nora. They're from Miami. Bud's retired now, but he used to be in the extermination business. Bugs, you know. You kill rodents, too, Bud?" she asked.

"Only the four-legged kind," Bud returned to much laughter.

"Bud, this here is my friend Calvin—"

"Cal," he interrupted her.

"And we met him on the bus from the airport," the woman barreled right on. "This is his friend... I'm sorry, dear. I didn't catch your name."

"Faith. Faith Bishop."

"How nice to meet you, Faith. I'm Gloria Steinheim, but no relation. To that *Ms.* woman... the feminist lady, you know?"

Faith nodded, trying to follow Gloria's abrupt change of subject.

"Not that I'm against women's rights," Gloria continued. "I was a riveter during the war. World War II, you know. They called me Glory in those days 'cause I had red hair. You can call me Glory, too. All my friends do. Sit, Calvin. No sense standing on ceremony here.''

Cal was tempted to make his excuses briskly and get the hell out of there, but the knowing look he saw in Faith's eyes stopped him. She'd gotten him into this mess on purpose, the little witch, and he could just about read her mind. She thought she had him between a rock and a hard place. Well, hell, two could play at that game.

''I'd love to join you, Glory,'' Cal said with his most dazzling smile. ''My friend here is a magazine editor. Maybe she could put a piece in her magazine about your days as a riveter.''

That was the only impetus Glory needed. Faith spent the next forty-five minutes—from appetizers of smoked salmon through soup, a delicious gazpacho, to the main course and beyond—listening to the story of Gloria's life.

When Glory finally had to stop to draw breath, the Kecks jumped in. ''Ah, those were the days,'' Nora Keck said. ''I met my honeybear at a USO dance. He was going to be shipped soon.''

''She means shipped *out*,'' Bud inserted.

''Of course I do, honeybear.'' Tilting her head to laugh at her husband, the dangling wooden cherry earrings Nora wore bobbed wildly. The matching cherry necklace stood out like a beacon against Nora's white jumpsuit, the fruit's vivid color an identical match to the equally bright red of her lipstick. The woman patted her husband's cheek fondly, her bracelet jingling merrily. ''Where else would you be shipped but *out?* Anyway, we were married two weeks later. And here we are, celebrating our fiftieth wedding anniversary.''

''Has it really been that long, fruitcup?''

''You bet, honeybear.''

''Guess it's true what they say. Time really does fly when you're having fun. But look,'' Bud said, pointing at Faith's dinner dish. ''We haven't let this poor girl finish her meal. We're already done with dessert and she's still on her prime rib.''

"We'll leave you and Cal in peace, then," Nora declared. "Come along, honeybear. Glory, you and your friend join us, too. We're heading for the casino." When Glory hesitated, Nora added, "That's where the men are."

"In that case, I think we will join you two," Glory immediately replied.

Seconds later, Faith and Cal found themselves alone at the table.

"I'd say we were about even now," Cal declared with a grin.

Faith feigned ignorance. "I have no idea what you're talking about. I enjoyed hearing Glory's stories." That much was the truth. "In fact, she gave me a great idea for an article. There is a renewed interest in the 1940s and I think Glory's story would be a wonderful human interest feature."

"Yeah, right. Eat your dinner."

Faith sighed and eyed him with an all-too-familiar exasperation. "Cal, I already have a father. I don't need another one."

"What's that supposed to mean?" he demanded, stealing a cherry tomato off her plate.

"It means that I don't need you telling me what to do."

"You're sure touchy today. You must have your period," he declared. "That's why you're acting so strange."

Faith almost choked.

"Hey, don't look so surprised," he said, patting her on the back in an attempt to be helpful. "I'm an enlightened guy. I lived in a coed dorm for four years, remember? I know all about PMS."

"Then you know that it can be used as a defense in a murder charge," Faith retorted. "I've got a steak knife in my hand, Cal. Don't tempt me to use it. And stop pounding my back as if I were a defective vending machine."

Cal did as she asked, leaning back to grin at her. This was the Faith he wanted to see. The fiery one. "If you don't have your period, then what *is* your problem?"

You are, she was tempted to say, but didn't want to admit it out loud. Doing so would only give Cal more power over her, and that was something she was trying to minimize. So she chose to tell herself that her edginess was due to the fact that she hadn't gotten enough sleep last night.

It didn't work. Okay, so Cal was also her problem, she admitted, but one she could deal with. When she and Chris had originally booked this trip through their travel agent—the one who'd recommended the trip insurance that Faith and Chris hadn't seen the need for at the time—the agent had assured them that no one spent much time in their cabin on a cruise. There was simply too much going on elsewhere. You only went to your cabin to sleep.

Sleep? Right. Three feet from Cal? Who was she kidding, Faith thought to herself a few hours later as she heard Cal singing a Fleetwood Mac song in the shower.

Faith made the most of her momentary privacy by quickly discarding her clothes and exchanging them for her satin pajamas. Hurriedly sliding into bed, she turned off her reading light and faced the wall. She figured if she couldn't *see* Cal, he wouldn't be able to bother her.

Wrong. She discovered that the moment he opened the bathroom door. She could smell the scent of his tangy soap. She could hear him breathing; hear the pad of his bare feet as he came closer.

Faith tensed, pretending to be sound asleep. She stayed that way for so long, her side grew numb. Eventually, she had to move or risk permanent damage. She rolled over to her other side as if she were still asleep. She kept her eyes shut, but the speculation was driving her nuts.

Just one peek, what could it hurt? It might even help. Maybe Cal had developed a beer belly. Or maybe he'd look ridiculous in pajama bottoms. She sneaked a look through her lashes.

He was only twelve inches away from her, close enough for her to see him despite her nearsightedness. Close enough for her to see the ripple of his back muscles as he tugged back the top sheet. She could see the way his pajama bottoms rode low on his hips. She couldn't see him as clearly as she would have liked, however, so she squinted to get a better look.

"Want your glasses?" Cal asked without turning around.

"Wha-at?" she sputtered.

"To get a better look."

"I was asleep," she informed him with a yawn. "Why would I want my glasses while I was sleeping?"

"You were peeping, not sleeping."

"You're imagining things."

"So are you," he drawled teasingly. "All kinds of things."

She wanted to throw her pillow at him, hit him broadside with it. He'd never see it coming....

As if able to read her thoughts, Cal turned around. "I wouldn't if I were you," he warned her.

In a huff, she turned over and faced the wall again.

Cal was amazed at her ability to be frosty with just the tip of one shoulder. Just about everything else was covered up with the sheets she'd tugged up to her nose. He stared at the back of her head, noticing that her hair was caught beneath the pajama top's collar, as if she'd tugged the garment on in a hurry. He had the strangest urge to reach out and free those trapped curls. Sighing, Cal sat on the edge of her bed.

"Hey, kid, relax, would you?" He frequently called her kid, even though she was only a year younger than he was. When she'd challenged him about it once, he'd teasingly informed her that she was light-years younger than he in experience. Despite the fact that she'd been married and divorced, he still felt that way about her. She had an inherent things-will-get-better attitude that he, cynic that he was, secretly admired. "If you don't relax, it's going to be a very, very long week."

She pretended not to hear him.

"I mean it's not as if you haven't shared a bedroom with a man before. You *were* married."

"That was different," she mumbled without turning over. "Albert was my husband."

"Albert was a jerk," Cal declared.

It was one thing for Faith to think Albert was a jerk, after having been married to him for a year, but it was another thing for Cal to say it. She sat up in bed and glared at him. "You didn't think Albert was a jerk when I married him."

"Sure I did, but I didn't think you'd appreciate hearing my opinion at the time."

"I don't appreciate hearing your opinion now, either. I can do without your telling me that I chose to marry a jerk, thank you very much. Like you're an expert on the subject of matrimony," she scoffed. "You, the man who can't even say the word *commitment* without breaking into a cold sweat. The man who claims *marriage* isn't a word, it's a sentence—and a long one at that."

"Did you know that when you get mad, your face gets all red," Cal noted, studying her as if she were a specimen in a petri dish.

"When I'm mad, I also get violent," she warned him darkly. "So you'd better get off my bed."

"So you can eye me again?" Cal inquired as he obligingly got up. "Hey, always happy to accommodate a friend."

"You want to accommodate me, go sleep down the hallway!"

"No can do, sweetheart. We're in this together. For better or worse."

Which left Faith with the sinking feeling that things were going to get much worse before they got any better.

Three

Faith woke the next morning to the sound of something hitting the outer bulkhead of the ship. "What was that?" she asked Cal in alarm.

A soft snore was his only reply.

"Lot of help you are," Faith muttered, getting up from her bed to peer out the porthole. The day was overcast, and to her blurred vision it looked as if the misty sky, the land and the water were all as one. Grabbing her glasses from the nightstand, she looked again. It was six-thirty in the morning and they were cruising past glaciers, alone in a world of white ice. The sound Faith had heard was from floating chunks of ice hitting the side of the ship.

"Cal, look!"

"I'm looking," he huskily assured her, eyeing the curve of her bottom in the unexpectedly sexy satin pj's Faith was wearing as she leaned forward, her nose almost pressed against the glass of the porthole.

Sexy? Cal reflected in sleepy confusion. He'd never thought of Faith as sexy before. Prickly, yes. Loyal as the day was long, for sure. She could even be cold as ice on occasion, when she was really ticked off. But sexy? He must be dreaming. This was Faith, he reminded himself. College buddy. The realization that his buddy happened to have a curvaceous derriere as well as a lovely pair of breasts made him feel decidedly uneasy. The seductive shadow of her cleavage above the first button on the open V neckline of her top didn't help matters, either.

"There's ice out here!" Faith said.

"We *are* in Alaska, kid." His use of her nickname was deliberate, a reminder of who she was and what their relationship had always been.

"Very funny, Masters. I'm telling you, we're sailing through ice here...not water."

"Physically impossible," Cal retorted with what he hoped looked like a lazy yawn. "You can't sail through ice."

Infuriated by his patronizing attitude, Faith grabbed Cal by the arm, yanked him out of bed and pointed out the porthole. "Look for yourself! And listen..." Another thunk echoed through the outer wall of their cabin. "What are those...baby icebergs?"

Instead of answering, Cal merely said, "Sure hope you know how to swim, kid."

"You think we're in trouble?" Faith asked in concern, turning her face up to his as if seeking reassurance.

Trouble? Her question hit Cal like a sucker punch in the gut. So did the surprising loveliness of her face, still flushed from what he assumed was the excitement of finding icebergs outside her porthole window. She had the peaches-and-cream complexion a lot of women he knew would kill for. Smooth, soft and fresh.

Had her eyes always been so wide and wondrous? They glowed with emotion while her hair fell in glorious waves around her shoulders, making her look like a Botticelli angel.

Hell, what was the matter with him? He and Faith had taken Art History together. He'd sailed a paper airplane at her while they'd studied for that exam together. He hadn't noticed her looking like a Botticelli angel then.

Glancing away from her, Cal rubbed his eyes and tried to get his chaotic thoughts in order. Needing a bit more time to pull his act together, he added a lazy stretch to get the cricks out of his spine. When he did finally look back at her, Cal heaved a visible sigh of relief to see she'd gone back to just being Faith again, and not some tousle-haired, wide-eyed nymph.

"Nah, we're not in trouble," Cal declared, as if reassuring himself of that fact, too. "But I'd pay attention to the lifeboat drill this morning if I were you," he added with casual wickedness before heading for the bathroom.

Alone, Faith tried telling herself that her inner trembling was due to her uncertainty about the prudence of sailing through what looked, to her, like solid slush. But she had a sinking feeling that her reaction was more a result of the sight of a bare-chested Cal stretching like a tawny lion. With her glasses on, she'd been able to see the sleek ripple of his every muscle.

When she'd taken anatomy in college, Cal had once teasingly offered his body for her to write the names of all the major muscle groups on. She'd replied with an equally teasing comment about waiting for him to develop further and grow into those muscles first. He certainly had.

Hearing the sound of an electric razor, she remembered the golden shadow gilding his strong jawline this morning. And then she remembered another morning... and another, younger Cal. She smiled at the recollection. Junior year in college. Six in the morning. She'd just opened the bathroom door and found Cal standing in the hallway, telling her he needed her help.

Before she'd been able to ask him for details, she'd heard the ominous rumble of someone approaching. Someone very, very big and very, very angry. Someone yelling Cal's name along with a string of inventive threats.

An instinctive need to protect Cal had taken hold. Grabbing a handful of Cal's T-shirt, Faith had yanked him into the bathroom with her and closed the door. Locking it, she'd motioned Cal to be quiet. When things had calmed down out in the hallway, she'd opened the bathroom door only to be confronted by the angry bruiser from the wrestling team who was still looking for Cal, apparently furious with him for "flirting with my little gal."

Since Faith had happened to know that the wrestler's "little gal" was the biggest flirt on campus, she'd felt no compunction whatsoever about denying any knowledge of Cal's whereabouts and reading the wrestler the riot act for daring to storm into the dorm. "This bathroom is clearly marked For Women Only. Do you think I'm the kind of girl who'd have a man in here with me? Do you?" Startled by her attack, the wrestler had backed off.

Meanwhile, Cal, standing behind the bathroom door where she'd hurriedly stuffed him, hadn't been helping matters any with his mimicking impression of the bruiser standing outside the door. She'd had to bite her tongue to stop from laughing. Trust Cal to complicate matters. He couldn't just stand there and shut up. No, he'd had to add an element of danger, the danger of discovery if she were to crack up and start giggling uncontrollably.

Nothing was ever simple or easy with Cal. No, that wasn't true, she contradicted herself while grabbing some clothes from the closet. Talking to Cal had been easy. It was true that arguing with him was even easier. But they'd had some wonderfully long discussions in college, talks that had gone on all night—debating everything from Thomas Hardy's use of coincidence in his books, to the statewide variances on the legal drinking age and whether this should be federally controlled, to the depiction of women in history. When he wasn't saying something to deliberately set her off, he had some intriguing things to say.

In many ways, Cal was like a clam, she decided. Only instead of a hard shell, he used his mocking sense of humor to keep others at bay. It had been a long time since she'd gotten past that outer shell to the sometimes fascinatingly tender man inside. She wondered if he was still in there or if the things he'd seen and experienced during his many years as a journalist had served to harden that shell all the way to his soul.

Faith had to believe he was still in there. But she also had to remind herself that she wasn't the one to pry him open and find out. Because if Cal was a clam, she had the potential of being a baby seal in this scenario. As a contributor to Greenpeace, Faith was well aware of what hunters had done in the past to baby seals. The animals were too trusting, too vulnerable, which is why they'd needed and had gotten protection.

Faith knew what it meant to be too vulnerable. Which is why she'd had to develop her own means of protection, her own kind of camouflage. And that meant doing whatever was necessary to guard her heart.

"Bathroom's all yours," Cal said as he stood in the open doorway. "You gonna stand there all morning and daydream, or what?"

"I've given up daydreams," Faith declared.

"Is that so?" His voice was clearly amused.

"Absolutely."

"I'll believe it when I see it."

"I don't believe it...." Faith muttered two hours later, after hearing her name announced over the ship's loudspeaker system. "Great. I'll bet I've just become the first passenger in the history of this ship to ever flunk the lifeboat drill."

Okay, so she'd had her life vest on backward.... She'd hoped no one had noticed. But the announcement, "Would Faith Bishop please call extension 561" hadn't sounded too reassuring.

Letting herself into her cabin, Faith immediately began undoing the stupid vest that no one was allowed to take off until reaching their quarters. The officer at the assembly point had been firm about that, explaining that someone might trip on the long fastening tabs.

Personally, Faith thought it more likely you'd bounce into and off of the hallway walls wearing the dumb thing. It was humongous and had huge blocks of the plastic stuff computers were packed in. Not a real glamorous fashion statement.

Cal, of course, had looked fine in his life vest and had come down to the cabin ahead of her, before taking off to check out the casino on board. Thankfully, Faith had the cabin to herself when she exchanged the bulky life vest for the clunky phone on the bedside table.

Extension 561 turned out to be the radio room. "We have a phone call for you from the mainland," Faith was told. "Hold on, please." She heard a few clicks and then, "Faith? Is that you? It's Chris."

"Chris! Are you all right? Has something else happened?"

"No. Aside from me breaking my leg, things are relatively quiet around here."

"Good. I'm sorry about your leg. I wish you were here instead of Cal. I can't believe you sold your ticket to him, of all people."

"Listen, Faith," Chris stated in no uncertain terms, "it's time you got over this thing you have for Cal."

"I do not have a *thing* for Cal," Faith denied.

"I saw the way you looked at him when he was in the hospital at Christmas. It's the same way I eye chocolate even though I know I can't have it because I'm allergic to it. You've gotta get him out of your system."

"I haven't been pining away for him, by any means," Faith retorted. "I have been getting on with my life. Dating."

"Speaking of dating, how are things going with you and Nigel?"

Nigel Lawrence was an Englishman, an investment broker Faith had been seeing for the past three or four months. "Things have been going fine," Faith replied. "Actually, Nigel wants us to move on to the next level in our relationship."

"Meaning he wants to go to bed with you," the ever-blunt Chris translated.

"Yes."

"What do *you* want?"

"I don't know. Nigel is giving me some time and space to make a decision. I was hoping to do that on this cruise. I thought that getting away would help me make up my mind."

"It will," Chris promised. "Seeing Cal in such close quarters, his dirty socks tossed all over the room—it's bound to put an end to your crush once and for all."

Faith laughed. "You know it did occur to me that you might have been acting as a matchmaker here," she admitted, "putting Cal and I together this way."

"Quite the opposite," Chris said. "While I certainly didn't break my leg on purpose, it did occur to me that maybe some good might come out of this—like your finally getting Cal out of your system. Remember that where romance is concerned, familiarity breeds contempt and absence makes the heart grow fonder. Cal's absence those seven years made you want him more. The two of you being cooped up together in that cabin should put an end to that. Look at it this way, here's your chance to get over Cal so you can live happily ever after with Nigel."

"You're just a sucker for an English accent," Faith said with a smile.

"You've got that right. Listen, don't get me wrong. I love Cal. As a friend, he's great. The best. But in a romantic relationship, he'd be…kind of lousy. You know how he is, Faith."

"I know." Faith realized that Cal avoided long-term romantic entanglements like the plague.

"Promise me you'll think about what I said. This is your chance to get cured, Faith. Grab it."

"Did you accomplish mission?" Ivan asked Natasha as she hurriedly entered the cabin.

"Of course," Natasha replied. "Did you?"

"Of course."

"Good. Purser said person who had our bag was on this deck. So diamonds must be on this deck."

"What if person has taken diamonds out of face-cream jar and put elsewhere?" Ivan said.

"Do not look for trouble. We will cross bridges when we get there."

"Bridges? What bridges?" Ivan demanded in confusion.

"Is American saying," Natasha replied. "You are certain no one saw you using secret device on door locks? No one saw you entering cabins?"

"Am certain no one saw. Was clever idea, to break into cabins during lifeboat drill. Peoples were all on deck and cabins were empty. Am glad I thought of idea."

"Was *my* idea," Natasha declared. "Your idea was to steal all jars of face cream in all cabins on this level. My idea was to do job while peoples are in lifeboat drill."

"So many jars..." Ivan shook his head in amazement as he looked at their stash of stolen containers.

"This jar is not face cream. Label says makes age spot disappear," Natasha said, holding it up to show him.

"Maybe also makes diamonds disappear," Ivan huffed. "Look in jar."

Natasha did. "No diamonds."

"Try next jar. Diamonds must be here somewhere..."

"What was that all about?" Cal asked, nodding toward the phone Faith had just hung up.

"What are you doing back here?" Faith countered. "I thought you were in the casino."

"It doesn't open until later this afternoon. I heard you being paged over the loudspeaker system and wondered what was up. What did you do?"

"I didn't do anything," Faith denied.

"Come on, Faith. They don't announce people's names for the hell of it."

"There was a phone call for me."

"Who was it?"

"Chris."

"So she called you, huh? I was wondering how long it would take her to do that."

"She was just calling to make sure . . ." Faith paused to search for the best words.

"To make sure we didn't kill each other," Cal supplied.

"Something like that."

The speculative way Faith was looking at him made Cal uneasy. What had she and Chris been concocting this time? "So what are you two up to now?" he demanded.

"Why do you think we're up to anything?" Faith asked with a look of utter innocence that didn't fool him for one minute.

"Because neither one of you could play poker worth a damn. You're no good at bluffing."

"Oh, I wouldn't say that," she said with an arch of her eyebrow.

Where had she learned to do that? Cal wondered. It made her look like a nymph again. He didn't like it. Not one bit. Faith had no right turning into a woman at this point in their relationship.

"You and Chris are up to no good," Cal declared. "I can tell. Remember the time you two decided to sneak a boa constrictor into the dorm?"

"That snake happened to be a pet," Faith reminded him.

"I knew then that both of you were planning something."

"I can assure you that Chris didn't break her leg to get you on this cruise," Faith said, just in case he was in any doubt.

"I never thought she did," Cal returned. "Even *she* wouldn't go to that extreme. You're not going to tell me what you're up to, are you?"

"Nope," she replied with a satisfied grin. Cal sounded aggravated. Good. Chris's call had renewed Faith's confidence. Being in the driver's seat with Cal was a tantalizing proposition. To have him out of her system once and for all. To get rid of the ridiculous case of nerves that tied her tongue in knots. To be able to meet him as an absolute equal. Yeah, that had real appeal.

"Fine," Cal said. "You and Chris can have your little secrets. You were probably talking about a man, anyway."

"That's right," Faith confirmed. "We were talking about Nigel."

"Who's Nigel? Some new guy Chris is seeing?"

How typical of Cal, Faith silently noted with displeasure. Since he didn't see her as a woman, he assumed other men didn't, either. Well, he was in for a surprise. "No, some new guy *I'm* seeing," she retorted. Did Cal have to look so damn surprised? Faith's aggravation level rose another notch or two.

"Oh, yeah? What's he do?"

"He's a very successful investment broker. And he could very well turn out to be Mr. Right where I'm concerned." Faith relished the stunned look on Cal's face right before she sashayed out of the cabin, delighted to be the one to finally have the last word for a change.

"Uh-oh. I recognize that look. You and your beau have a fight?" Glory asked Faith as the older woman dropped into a deck chair beside her an hour later.

After leaving the cabin, Faith had headed for the upper observation deck with her 35-mm camera in hand. Sitting there with the brisk, damp wind blowing on her face, she felt invigorated and inspired. She'd already taken half a roll of film. Although the day was still overcast, the clouds had lifted enough from this morning's fogginess in College Fjord for them to see most of the mountains, if not their actual peaks. "Cal isn't my beau," Faith automatically corrected Glory before taking a quick shot of the view through a life preserver hanging on the railing. She was pleased with the composition and hoped it would develop into a perfect picture.

"Not your beau, huh?" Glory repeated. "Then what do you call them these days...let me think...um...I've got it!'' Glory snapped her fingers. "Your significant other, right?" she said proudly.

"He isn't that, either." Faith rested her camera in her lap and turned her full attention to Glory. "You don't understand. Our relationship is strictly platonic."

"That doesn't stop you from fighting, does it?"

"No."

"So you two *did* have a fight. I knew it. I can always tell these things." Turning her head, Glory yelled out to her friend who stood farther down at the guardrail, looking for bald eagles through a pair of binoculars. "Hey, Rhoda, I was right! They had a fight. I told you so." Glory then turned back to Faith again and patted Faith's hand. "There now, tell me all about it, dear."

"We didn't have a fight. Really, Gloria, there's nothing to tell."

"Call me Glory, dear. You can trust me. I'm the soul of discretion."

Faith had to smile at that misnomer. "I'm sure you are. Is this your first cruise, Glory?" she asked, eager to change the subject.

"Oh, no. This is our third. Rhoda and I love them. You meet such interesting people. This is our first time north, though. On our other cruises we visited the Caribbean islands. It's much chillier up here, isn't it?" Glory noted with a shiver.

"Hard to believe it's early June with all this snow and ice," Faith agreed.

"I was hoping for better weather," Glory said with a disparaging look at the overcast skies.

"You have to admit that this kind of weather makes the scenery look even more magical, though," Faith said. "I read somewhere that the blue color of the glaciers is actually heightened on cloudy days."

"I see you've got a camera with you."

Faith nodded. "I got some nice shots this morning when we were in College Fjord. I'm hoping they turn out."

"My, you must have been up bright and early this morning. We'd already left the fjord by the time I got up at nine."

"You could say I got a special wake-up call," Faith noted.

"Really?" Glory leaned forward, all ears.

Faith could tell by the other woman's eager expression that she'd misinterpreted her comment. "I was referring to the fact that the sound of the ice hitting the side of the ship this morning woke me up at six-thirty. Still, I was glad I woke up. The scenery was spectacular—"

"Wait a second," Glory interrupted. "You're telling me that ice was hitting the side of the ship this morning? Oh, my stars! You don't think we'll hit an iceberg and sink like the Titanic, do you? I knew someone who had a relative on that ship. I'll bet that's why we had that lifeboat drill this morning. Because we're sailing in dangerous waters. Now it makes sense. Icebergs! Why, just thinking about it is enough to scare the liver right out of you!"

"Honestly, Glory, I don't think the icebergs are a problem," Faith tried to reassure her. "They've got all kinds of modern navigational equipment now that they didn't have when the Titanic was sailing. And cruise ships sail these waters all the time."

"Not this early in the season," Glory maintained. "This is one of the first cruises of the season. That's why it was cheaper. Because you run the danger of hitting an iceberg. Sure, now it makes sense. They do the same in the Caribbean. Not with icebergs, of course. With hurricanes. In hurricane season, they lower the rates, too."

"That doesn't mean that you're going to sail into a hurricane," Faith observed. "You can see them coming with the forecasting technology available today, and the ships steer clear of that area then."

"Maybe. But how do you steer clear of an iceberg? Do you know?"

"Well, no, but—"

"I'm going to go speak to the ship's captain about it right now!" Glory declared.

Once she was gone, Faith left the deck chair behind in favor of returning to the guardrail. Lifting the camera she had around her neck, Faith focused her telephoto lens on a particularly brilliant patch of blue at the edge of the Columbia Glacier, which lay ahead of the ship.

Looking through the lens, she realized the gorgeous glacier-blue was the exact color of Cal's eyes. She lowered her camera in disgust. This was ridiculous. It had to stop. It would. Starting right now.

Chris was right. This cruise was Faith's chance for her to get Cal out of her system once and for all and, by God, she was going to do that—come hell or high water.

And so it was that an hour later, Faith was sitting in the observation lounge, toasting her newfound resolve to that old *South Pacific* classic, "I'm Gonna Wash That Man Right Outa My Hair." She'd put her contacts in again and had even bought a new pair of retro-designed sunglasses she'd seen in one of the ship's shops, donning a new confidence with them. After all, the sunglasses looked like something Bette Davis would have worn and *she* certainly hadn't lacked confidence.

The wind had whipped some of the curl out of Faith's perm and added color to her cheeks. Checking the mirrored wall across the lounge, she grinned at the picture she made. Not half-bad. Not bad at all. She almost didn't recognize herself.

Half of life was attitude, she decided. This afternoon, she had it. And it extended to the clothes she wore, which although new weren't glamorous. But when you had attitude, you didn't need glamour. You could turn jeans, a white T-shirt and a red buffalo-print flannel shirt into something special. All it took was confidence and a flick of a shirt collar here, a good fit in the jeans there, and a really spiffy pair of ankle boots. All in all, perfect "Northern Exposure" attire. Faith congratulated herself.

Sitting in the front of the observation lounge, she'd already ordered herself a drink with all the aplomb of a world traveler. She'd also handled the flirtatious attention of the Italian waiter with equal ease.

"I couldn't help but notice you sitting here on your own. Mind if I join you.... Oh, it's you," Cal said, sinking into the empty chair next to her.

Faith sighed. She'd been doing so well. She refused to let his appearing at her side deflate her balloon. Those days were over. "Yes, it's me. I thought we were going to stay out of each other's way."

"How did you get a drink so quickly?" he asked, ignoring her comment. "I've been sitting over there for ten minutes trying to get a waiter's attention."

"Really? I found Alberto to be very attentive," Faith noted with a Mona Lisa smile.

Cal looked at her suspiciously. First, Faith was arching an eyebrow and sashaying that morning, now she was smiling secretively. Something was definitely up here. "Alberto, huh? You didn't learn from your first Albert experience?"

"Alberto is nothing like my ex-husband."

"They share the same name, although this guy is more warm-blooded, I'll grant you that."

"How generous of you," Faith returned mockingly.

"Speaking of being generous, let me buy you a drink," he said, raising his hand and getting the waiter's attention so quickly that it belied his earlier claim.

"Why?" Faith asked suspiciously. "Why should you want to buy me a drink?"

"There has to be a reason? I'll have a beer, and give the lady a refill of whatever she's having," he told Alberto. To Faith he said, "You weren't at lunch."

"I decided to have lunch in the café instead of the dining room."

"Oh. What have you been doing all afternoon? I hope you haven't been avoiding me." Cal eyed her expectantly.

"Not at all," she replied honestly. "I was busy taking pictures. I got some great shots of the Columbia Glacier earlier. It just so happened that I was there while they were lowering a lifeboat with some of the crew members in it."

"Abandoning ship, were they?" Cal inquired sardonically, telling himself he was pleased she wasn't avoiding him. Wasn't he? There was definitely something different about her and he wished he could put his finger on what it was.

"They were collecting a piece of ice to use in an ice carving demonstration this afternoon," she was saying. "Having the lifeboat in the foreground put the hugeness of the glacier into perspective. I hope the shots turn out."

Faith's shots always turned out, Cal thought. They were damn good, in fact. So good that he'd submitted a few to a contest he'd read about. She'd been furious. But she'd come in second. They'd still been in college at the time.

Given her talent, he would have thought that it would be a toss-up whether she'd pursue photography as a career. But that wasn't how Faith saw things. "Photography is fun," she'd once told him. "I can do whatever I want without getting bogged down in technicalities. I just want to compose the picture and take it. That's it. So long as *I* like the shot, I'm happy."

So she'd gone into something else at which she'd always excelled—editing. In Cal's opinion, Faith had a way of getting to the heart of matters, just as she did in photography; stripping away the surface junk and finding a jewel hidden underneath. Back in the old days, she'd certainly been one of the best damn editors he'd ever had. She'd taught him a lot. She'd been able to see things he couldn't...

Cal frowned at this bout of nostalgia. It wasn't like him to dwell in the past. He certainly hadn't planned on it when he'd insisted on joining her.

When he'd first seen her across the room, he really hadn't recognized her. The trendy sunglasses had thrown him off guard. But the instant he'd gotten closer, he'd realized it was her. For one thing, he recognized the distinctive light rose scent of her perfume—rose water, she'd called it in college and had a fondness for it ever since. Still, even recognizing it was her, Cal had used his cover story, anyway. Made him feel more comfortable that way.

Besides, from a distance, all he'd noticed was the flash of her confident smile and the feminine curve of her denim-clad legs. Not that that admission sat easily with him. Because while there were a lot of things he admired about Faith—her intelligence, her talent, her humor, her spirit—he'd never admired her legs before. Not that he was about to start now. Faith was a friend. A buddy.

Cal would slug any guy who tried to take advantage of her. Faith wasn't the kind of woman you fooled around with. She was the kind of woman you married. Definitely not the kind of woman for a rambling man like him.

Several hours and countless jars of face cream later, Natasha looked at Ivan in frustration and said, "Is not here! Diamonds not here!" Jars of opened face cream surrounded them, their various scents filling the air with a sickly sweetness. "Now what do we do?"

"Give me minute to think," Ivan ordered, rubbing his dark mustache.

"You are *sure* curse is not true?" Natasha asked.

Ivan silenced her with a glare. Ignoring her question, he said, "We are dealing with clever persons here. Clever enough to steal diamonds from us. You say your bag was opened when you got it, yes?"

"Yes. I would never bunch favorite red robe in such a manner. Someone had been in bag."

"We checked out purser, yes?"

Natasha waved away that suggestion. "Was not purser. Trust me, I gave him sixth and seventh degree. He knows nothing."

"Except who had bag before us."

"There are other ways of finding out that information. I am not seducing purser again. Man has hands like squid."

Natasha shuddered. "Peoples on this ship gossip all the times. You noticed this, yes?"

Ivan nodded.

"Then we just listen to gossip about someone losing bag and we will find peoples who had our bag . . . and our diamonds."

"I'm telling you, it's gone," Faith told Cal as she got ready for dinner that night. "I had my face cream this morning and now it's gone."

"You probably just misplaced it," Cal said, sliding an already knotted tie over his head and tightening it around his collar.

"I didn't misplace it. Besides, I've looked everywhere. The bathroom, the drawers, even in my purse and the empty suitcases. Did you put it anywhere?"

"I haven't seen your face cream."

"There you go, then," she said as if that proved her hypothesis. "I'm telling you, this is really weird."

Her next comment was interrupted by an announcement over the loudspeaker, relayed in their cabin through the speaker in the bedside table's built-in radio. "This is your captain speaking. It has come to my attention that a number of passengers on Three Deck have reported missing jars of face cream. Would anyone with any knowledge of this face-cream incident please report directly to me at the captain's cocktail party this evening. Thank you and we hope you're enjoying your cruise."

"You see," Faith said triumphantly. "I told you something was wrong. We're on Three Deck!"

"Just because you lost your face cream—"

"I didn't lose it. Someone must have broken into our cabin while we were above deck this afternoon, enjoying the scenery."

Cal gave her a look that clearly said *Come on. Tell me another one.*

"Aren't you the least bit concerned about this?" she demanded.

"About someone stealing jars of face cream? Yeah, sure it concerns me. Means someone on this ship has some very strange taste."

Once again, his attitude galled her. "If anyone is strange on this ship, it's you."

"How did you jump to that wild conclusion?"

"Somebody breaks into our cabin and all you have to say is that they have strange taste? I don't believe you!"

"I don't believe anyone broke into our cabin and stole your face cream. Not when they didn't touch my notebook computer, a much more expensive item, you'll agree? Clearly, you must have misplaced your face cream."

"Oh? So now you're saying everyone on this deck misplaced their face cream?"

"No. I don't know what went on in anyone else's cabin. Only what went on here."

"Which you can tell even though you weren't in the cabin yourself."

"Anyone with half a brain could see that it doesn't make sense for someone to break in here and not touch anything valuable," he scoffed.

"So now you're insinuating that I have less than half a brain?"

"I wouldn't go quite that far. Let's just say that you tend to get hysterical about some things."

"I do not get hysterical," she said between clenched teeth.

"Sure you do. You're hysterical right now."

"That's not hysterical. THIS IS HYSTERICAL!" she shouted, whirling away from him.

"Of all the idiotic... Come back here." He grabbed for her and the impetus of his strength tumbled her straight into his arms. Clearly startled, Faith blinked up at him with those wondrous eyes of hers. Her creamy cheeks were flushed, her parted lips a mere millimeter from his.

Cal didn't think. He reacted. Before he knew what was happening, he was kissing her.

Four

―――

Faith was stunned. She wasn't prepared. She hadn't seen this coming and her defenses weren't in place yet.

Her mind scrambled to catch up, to no avail. Cal was kissing her. This couldn't be real. Could it? This must be how Alice felt when she'd dreamed she'd gone through the Looking Glass and ended up in Wonderland. Amazed and dazed. Excited and thrilled. Subconsciously aware that nothing would ever be the same again after this. Faith was unable to speculate further as her thoughts were inundated by the tidal wave of unadulterated pleasure washing over her.

Closing her eyes, Faith was instantly swept away by the magic. Cal's mouth was as incredibly tempting as Faith had dreamed. The kiss wasn't platonic and it wasn't polite. It was intense and earthy, sensual and direct. Their lips blended in stunning accord. There was no awkwardness. Only raw heat.

Fire. Faith was burning up with it. The flames were fueled by the seductive flick of his tongue as desire raced through her bloodstream like a tropical fever. Cal's hands were curled around her shoulders, but he wasn't holding her against her will. He didn't need to. The sheer force of his kiss had her immobilized...mesmerized...tantalized.

Her eyes fluttered open, only to shut again as her other senses opened to the flood of sensations. Warmth radiated from his body like heat off hot street pavement. She could feel it even through the flannel of her shirt, the thin cotton of her T-shirt. She instantly memorized the feel of his hands, of every individual finger curling around her shoulders. Her body recognized his touch and labeled it as belonging.

Her hands were spread open on his chest, as if to push him away when in fact they were taking pleasure in the contact as she hazily noted the beat of his heart beneath her right palm. She heard ragged breathing but didn't know if it was hers or his or a seductive mixture of both. She tasted the tangy mint of his toothpaste and recognized the clean scent of his after-shave.

She savored every detail and participated in every enticing exploration led by his tempting tongue. Farther and farther she fell, down the blissful rabbit hole of forgotten identities. Thoughts came in pulses. Racing heart. Hunger. Hers? His? Shallow breaths...theirs...who needed air?

She did. She was drowning here, cast adrift in a sea of sensation. She'd responded to his kiss with wanton honesty, parting her lips and swaying toward Cal like a plant seeking sunlight.

It had to stop. The order streaked through her brain but it took several moments and every ounce of willpower she possessed for her body to obey the command, *Protect yourself and move away. Now! Before you make a fool of yourself all over again!*

She didn't get very far. She couldn't. Her knees were shaking too badly.

Opening her eyes, Faith glanced at Cal, looking for something, a sign of how he felt. She didn't search for long. She couldn't. But she'd seen enough. Walls. He'd erected them. She needed to do the same, marshal her own defenses. Since Cal wasn't giving any of his thoughts away, she couldn't afford to give her own inner turmoil away, either.

So she plastered on a bright smile and said, "That will teach me to go two nights without enough sleep. When I'm exhausted, I get punchy," Faith stated with a fairly convincing, she thought, laugh. "I'd say we both got a bit carried away for a minute there. I was obviously missing Nigel. And you...well, you were angry. No big deal. Good thing we're friends and know it was just a freak occurrence. Oh my gosh, look at the time. I've got to change or I'm going to be late for the captain's cocktail party tonight. I wonder what I should wear," she mused, calmly— outwardly, at least—walking toward the closet to survey her wardrobe choices.

Cal was stung by her dismissal of what had just happened between them. Not that he knew what the hell that *was* that had just happened between them. Sex? Lust? What?

He'd kissed Faith. His old college buddy. The prickly peach, as they'd called her in college. Good ol' Faithful Faith.

Cal speared his fingers through his hair in an attempt to regain some of his famous control. "It was no big deal," he agreed. Faith had responded to him because he'd caught her by surprise and she was thinking of Nigel. God alone knew why *he'd* done what he'd done by kissing her in the first place, let alone responding and deepening the kiss.

Cal only knew he felt on very unsteady and shifting ground here. It wasn't a feeling he liked. And the truth was he wasn't wild about being used as a stand-in for her boyfriend, Mr. Right—Nigel whatever-his-name-was. "You go ahead and change. I'll see you around," Cal said with cheerful carelessness before leaving the cabin.

Half an hour later, Faith was dressed and ready for the cocktail party. Since the suggested dress for the occasion

was formal, Faith had chosen to wear something special.
The calf-length black silk taffeta full skirt was a recent ac-
quisition from one of Seattle's vintage clothing stores and
was very 1950s. The black velvet bodysuit top she wore with
it, with sheer net sleeves and lace trimming around the
sweetheart neckline, was very 1990s. Around her neck, she
wore one of her favorite pieces from her small collection of
Victorian jewelry, a delicate garnet teardrop necklace. She'd
pinned her hair on top of her head so that the bouncy curls
just barely tickled her nape.

She'd resolutely blocked Cal's kiss from her mind, and
had concentrated instead on looking her best. She also had
to concentrate on not poking her eye out with her mascara
brush. Not only was the movement of the ship hampering
her efforts, the trembling of her hands weren't helping
matters, either. She'd come so close to making a total idiot
of herself again. To melting in his arms and moaning her
pleasure.

Difficult though it had been, she'd pulled things—her
self respect and her pride—out of the fire just in the nick of
time. While no one liked making a fool of themselves and
leaving themselves open for ridicule, Faith was particularly touchy about it. She admitted as much. But she had
her reasons.

From the time she was a child, Faith had heard her
mother's horror stories about being left at the altar as a
nineteen-year-old bride-to-be. Her mother had never forgotten the humiliation. When she'd met Faith's father and
agreed to marry him, they'd had a quiet ceremony in a jus-
tice of the peace's office rather than having her mother face
the trauma of another spectacle.

Coming from a small town, where gossip was rife, her
mother had had to deal with the gossip for years afterward
and had been referred to as "that jilted Johnson girl" even
though she'd been married and been Mrs. Bishop for a
decade. To this day, her mother hated nothing worse than
drawing attention to herself.

Faith wasn't wild about being the center of that kind of attention, either. Having been ridiculed herself in grade school as "Four Eyes" and an ugly duckling, Faith had had her own taste of humiliation and she hadn't found it any more to her liking than her mother had. Then, of course, there was that disastrous New Year's Eve kiss...and the resulting embarrassment.

Faith shook her head. She'd done the right thing by lying to Cal, saying their kiss tonight hadn't meant anything. That she'd been thinking of someone else.

And hopefully, soon, it wouldn't be a lie. She *would* be thinking of Nigel...or someone—anyone but Cal. But Faith had to admit that so far her plan to get over Cal seemed to be backfiring in her face.

"As I was saying, Ivan, it's been an unsettling cruise so far," Glory declared, even more expansive than usual as a result of the delightful attention Ivan had been paying her the past few minutes. "Things have been going wrong. I don't like it one bit, I can tell you. First, that nice girl Faith got the wrong bag delivered to her room, and although the purser assured me that was the only mix-up that occurred with the luggage, who knows? And now there's this face-cream incident. We had some taken from our cabin as well, you know. What have things come to that we're not even safe from thieves on a cruise out here in the middle of nowhere? I know they said to put your valuables in safe-deposit boxes at the purser's office, but who'd have thought someone would want to steal face cream?"

"Thieves are everywhere," Ivan agreed with a disapproving shake of his head. "Peoples stealing valuables. Is very bad."

"Very bad, indeed." Smiling brilliantly, Glory continued, "You have a lovely accent, if you don't mind me saying so, Ivan. Where did you say you were from again?"

"Is too painful for me to talk about mother country," Ivan declared, pressing his hand against his heart as if he had some deep wound there.

"I understand." Glory gently patted his hand. "I'm no stranger to pain myself."

"Tell me more about nice girl Faith," Ivan said.

"Oh, you continental men are all alike. An eye for the ladies, hmm?" Glory noted with a flirtatious bat of her false eyelashes. "I do believe Faith is already taken, however, Ivan. Her name is Faith Bishop and she was eating dinner with her handsome young man last night. Not that you're not good-looking in your own way, Ivan," Glory quickly added. "Faith may have said that she and Cal Masters were only friends, but they *are* sharing the same cabin and I saw the way she was looking at him.... Ivan? Now where did that man go off to in such a hurry?" Glory muttered.

Lost in the crowd, Ivan joined Natasha, who was sitting at the bar. Quickly tugging her off the bar stool, he crooked his finger for her to bend down so he could whisper in her ear. "I know woman's name. One who had our bag. Is Faith Bishop. She must have our... valuables."

"Excellent, Ivan."

"And she shares cabin with man—"

"Named Cal Masters," Natasha completed in a whisper. "I know. I spoke to couple from Miami. They have very strange names. Honeybear and fruitbag, or something. Is no matter. They told me what we needed to know. Now we have suspects. I will examine him. You befriend woman."

"I will use my continental charm on her," Ivan declared.

"And I will use my sex appeal on him," Natasha stated with a careless swish of her long, dark hair. "Do not worry, Ivan. We will get valuables back *very* soon."

"Hello, big boy," Natasha murmured as she sidled up to Cal. "Have you got fire in your pocket?"

Cal almost choked on the Scotch he was drinking. "What?"

She dangled her unlit cigarette at him meaningfully.

"Oh, a light," Cal belatedly translated. "Sure. Here...."

"Thank you." Natasha blew a thin stream of smoke out of her blood-red mouth before asking in a sultry undertone, "Want to buy me drink?"

"Why not. Name your poison."

"Poison?" Natasha repeated in alarm. "Was not me. I did not use poison. Is vicious lie!"

"I meant what kind of drink would you like?" Cal clarified.

"Oh. Vodka. Big glass."

"You got it."

"No—" Natasha looked at Cal in confusion "—I do not have drink."

"I'll get it for you and be right back."

"Good. Hurry, big boy. I have big plans for us...."

Faith watched Cal talk to the slinky brunette with the long hair. This was why she had to get over him. Because he had awful taste in women. Look at the getup the woman was wearing—a black leather jacket and pants more suited for a biker's rally than a cocktail party. And the leather was so tight she couldn't possibly be wearing underwear beneath it. To top it all off, the jacket was unzipped almost to the woman's navel. Tacky. Obvious and tacky. No class.

Faith prided herself on having plenty of class. She preferred her men to have it, too. She liked them charming and worldly. In that respect, Ivan, the foreign gentleman she'd just met, reminded her a bit of Nigel, although Nigel was much better-looking and a number of years younger. There *was* such a thing as continental charm, however. Knowing how to treat a lady. Something Cal had clearly never learned, despite his having traipsed all over the world. You'd never see Cal kissing a lady's hand.

Kissing... The memory of him kissing her was difficult to get out of her head. Temporary insanity. On both their parts. Or anger. People did strange things when they were angry, said things they didn't mean, did things they didn't

mean to do. Cal hadn't meant to kiss her any more than
she'd meant to kiss him back.

"You must not look so sad, Faith," Ivan said. "You are
much too lovely to be sad."

"Thank you." She was flattered and surprised by his
comment.

"Is true. In my country, a woman such as you would
have long line of admirers."

"That's very kind of you to say. I'm sorry, but I didn't
catch where you're from. Where exactly is your country?"

"Out there." Ivan flung out his hand, almost knocking
over a tray of hors d'oeuvres from a passing waiter. "I
cannot speak of it. Is too painful."

"I'm sorry. I wasn't trying to pry. Is this your first
cruise?"

"Yes. And you?"

"Mine, too," Faith replied.

"Ah, something we have in common, no? Perhaps we
could share dinner tomorrow and you could tell me more
about life in your United States."

Seeing Cal laughing at the slinky dragon lady, Faith said,
"I'd be delighted to do that, Ivan."

He beamed at her. "Good. Very good."

"Faith, there's someone I'd like you to meet," Glory interrupted them, indicating the uniformed officer she'd just
dragged over to join them. "This is John Wood. He's the
ship's navigator and he made me feel ever so much better
about those nasty icebergs out there. I thought you might
want to talk to him...you know, interview him for that
magazine of yours."

Faith didn't bother pointing out that she wasn't a re-
porter for the magazine, she was its senior editor. Writers
and assistant editors pitched their story ideas to her. She
didn't do any interviewing herself. The writers she hired did
that.

But the navigator's English accent reminded Faith of
Nigel, so Faith's smile was extra warm as she greeted him.
She also recognized him as the officer at the captain's ta-

ble who had given her such an appreciative look that first night.

"Come along, Ivan. Let's leave these two youngsters alone." Glory transferred her no-nonsense hold from the navigator's arm to Ivan's.

There was no way Ivan could protest without causing a scene, something Natasha had drummed into his head not to do. So he left, happy in the knowledge that he would be having dinner tomorrow night with the woman who would lead him to the diamonds.

"Here's your vodka, uh, I didn't catch your name," Cal admitted while handing her the drink.

"I am Natasha."

"Well, Natasha, I'm Cal. And I'm glad to meet you." Cal figured he needed some distraction about now. He didn't want to think about what had happened when he'd kissed Faith. He didn't want to remember the sweet indulgence of her mouth.

Yep, Cal decided. Natasha was just what he needed. She and Faith were like night and day. Opposites. Natasha was much more like the kind of woman he was normally attracted to—not that he was attracted to Faith, he hurriedly denied to himself.

"So, you enjoying this cruise?" Cal asked the exotic Natasha.

"Enjoying much more now that I have met you," she replied with a look guaranteed to increase the size of a man's ego.

Cal gave her one of his knock'em-dead grins, but it faded as he caught sight of Faith over Natasha's shoulder. His college buddy, dressed to the nines, was on the other side of the room, talking and laughing with one of the officers. Who the hell was *he*? And what the hell was he doing with his arm around Faith?

"Sorry about that," Faith apologized, after almost losing her balance. She was grateful to John for saving her from stumbling. "Is it my imagination, or are things getting bumpier here? Honestly, I've only had three sips of wine, so it isn't me," she assured him with a grin.

"It isn't you. We're out in the open ocean now," John replied. "We've left the protection of the bay, so it might get a little rougher now. But the ship is equipped with stabilizers."

As the ship made another bucking move, Faith hung on to his arm. "Doesn't feel like they're working." Looking around, she noticed a number of people making a hurried departure, looking more than a little green around the gills. "It's a good thing I don't get seasick."

"They have those patches now to cure seasickness," John noted.

"Is that what those are? I noticed a lot of the passengers wearing them."

"They can make things easier."

Faith and the officer chatted a few more minutes before he said, "If you have the time, perhaps we could have a drink together after dinner tonight."

"That would be lovely," Faith replied. "Thank you."

Two invitations in one evening, Faith thought to herself with a grin. Exactly what she needed to keep her mind off Cal.

By the time the second seating for dinner was announced, it was eight-thirty and things were definitely getting rougher, in more ways than one. The ship was bouncing around much more than it had before, so much so that it was difficult to walk. Tricky, might be a better word for it, Faith decided, carefully putting her foot down. The floor had a tendency to move, to be closer or farther than it had been a second before. Rather like the time the optometrist had given her the wrong prescription for her glasses. She hadn't been able to judge the distance to the floor then, either.

She also wasn't able to judge what Cal was thinking as he walked ahead of her, listening to Glory. He'd put on a jacket and tie in honor of the cocktail party. She tried to look at him objectively. There were other men on board who were better-looking, who were taller, who had broader shoulders. Cal was just a man.

A man whose kiss made her lose her reason it was true, but just a man, nonetheless. He was the antithesis of Nigel. Nigel was much more like John Wood—a civilized, cultured man of the world. A man with class and savvy. A man whose kisses were . . . nice. Fine. Very nice.

Faith sighed. This was getting complicated.

A second later, it got even more complicated as Faith pitched into Cal after the ship lurched yet again. His hands burned through the sheer net of her sleeves. It was the first time he'd touched her since kissing her. Awareness sizzled through her, making her feel even more unbalanced than the tossing of the ship did.

"Looks like we're sailing into some choppy waters," Cal said.

"You can say that again," Faith muttered. The choppiness wasn't only outside the ship, it was also inside her. She could only hope she'd maneuver her way through the rough patches more smoothly than the ship was currently doing.

"So, how did mission go?" Natasha asked Ivan the moment she entered their cabin after dinner. "Ivan? Ivan, where are you?"

"In bathroom," Ivan faintly replied.

"You sound strange. Something is wrong?"

A green-looking Ivan opened the bathroom door. "You were not at dinner. You drank too much vodka at party?" Natasha asked in an accusatory way.

Ivan glared at her and held on to the doorframe with a two fisted grip in order to stay upright. "Was not vodka! I can drink bottles of vodka with no effect. Is ship!"

"Ship?" Natasha repeated, not understanding.

"Ship is moving. Making me ocean-ill."

"Seasick," Natasha corrected him. "I told you to read English dictionary while we are here. You must improve language skills."

Ivan glared at her. "I am not reading dictionary! Reading makes me ill when moving."

Natasha ignored his comment. "What did you discover about missing diamonds?"

"I am meeting with woman tomorrow," Ivan replied.

"When? Morning? Evening?"

Instead of answering, Ivan just nodded and then groaned.

Natasha ventured a guess. "You are meeting for dinner?"

The mention of food made Ivan's complexion even greener. "Do not talk food to me. Is cruel."

"Poor Ivan. You want I should bring you something?"

"Bring me new stomach." With that strangled request, Ivan headed back into the bathroom.

"Well, this is another fine mess I've gotten myself into," Faith muttered to herself as she punched her pillow into a more comfortable shape. While doing so, she couldn't help but notice that the time displayed on the bedside digital clock was almost three a.m.

There was no sign of Cal. After a dinner fraught with tension and meaningful silences, Cal took off, muttering something about going to play blackjack and how she shouldn't wait up for him.

As if she would. But who could sleep with the boat...*ship*, she corrected herself, with the ship bouncing around like a cork in a white-water river. Since their cabin was near the bow, it tended to pitch up and down more than the rest of the ship.

Faith told herself she was glad to be left on her own for a while. It gave her the chance to mentally review all the things she liked about Nigel and disliked about Cal. Problem was, she couldn't seem to get her thoughts in order. Instead, they kept veering off into forbidden territory—like remembering the feel of Cal's hand on her arm when he'd saved her from falling right before dinner.

The navigator had saved her from falling, too, but his touch hadn't affected her. Cal's had. So what was she doing wrong here? Why wasn't her plan to get over Cal working yet? It wasn't for lack of desire. She groaned at her use of that word. What she'd meant was that she truly wanted to get over Cal. She didn't enjoy being this vulnerable. She wanted to laugh off his teasing. She also wanted to be a size ten, but there didn't appear to be any sign of that happening in the near future, either!

Faith sighed and punched her pillow again, hanging on to the side of the bed with her other hand. She didn't want to end up on the floor. She didn't want to end up humiliated by a man the way her mother had been, either. She just wanted to be cured, wanted to be over Cal. Surely that wasn't too much to ask?

"Tomorrow is another day," she told herself, regardless of the fact that it already *was* tomorrow, and there was still no sign of Cal.

"Listen to this," Glory said as she joined Faith in the Outrigger Café for lunch. "There is a singles champagne party this afternoon at one. Sounds like fun."

Glory was reading from the *Daily Program* newsletter, which the purser slid under each cabin's doorway every morning. Seeing the newsletter, Faith recalled a bleary-eyed Cal tossing his in the wastebasket that morning after almost slipping on the sheet of paper. "It's too early for the sun to be up," he'd growled.

"According to the program you just threw out, sunrise was at 4:22 a.m."

"I didn't get to bed until four."

Faith had noticed that fact, but she made no comment. This grumbling Cal was one she could cope with. It reminded her of the old Cal, the safer one, and the times she'd beaten him hands down at Ping Pong. He'd been disgruntled then, too.

And so, to her relief, there had been no reference to their kiss of yesterday evening. Instead, she and Cal had both acted as if nothing had happened. Not that this was an entirely new occurrence for Faith. After all, she'd done the same thing years before, after that New Year's Eve kiss. She'd put on a great act, covering up those old childhood feelings of being inferior—not good enough, not thin enough, not glamorous enough.

Faith was older and wiser now, although still not glamorous in the usual sense of the word, she admitted wryly. But she'd come to value her differences, rather than to worry about them. That didn't mean she was any more eager to make a fool of herself now than she'd been at age twenty-one, however. It just meant that she'd learned to like herself, and to try to accept herself for who she was and what she'd accomplished.

So she'd had a momentary setback on her road to recovery with Cal. That didn't mean she wouldn't ultimately be successful. Faith reminded herself that she had lots of options. Nigel waiting for her back in Seattle was a definite possibility. She simply had to acknowledge that Cal wasn't a possibility for anything other than friendship and then she'd be over him once and for all. Surely their platonic attitude that morning was a step in the right direction?

"Perhaps Ivan will be there," Glory was saying. "What do you think?" Glory looked at Faith expectantly.

"What do I think about what?" Faith murmured, her thoughts still on her recovery.

"About Ivan."

"Ivan? He seems a nice man."

"For me," Glory said meaningfully. "Yes, I thought so, too. He's really too old for you, my dear. Now, that nice navigator is much better for you."

Faith couldn't hide her amusement. "Is that why you brought him over yesterday evening at the cocktail party?"

"I saw the two of you having drinks after dinner last night. But then he got up suddenly. You two didn't have a fight, did you? You're already fighting with Cal."

"I'm not fighting with Cal," Faith denied.

"The two of you were awfully quiet at dinner. But getting back to that nice navigator..."

"He was called back to the bridge," Faith said. "That's why he left early."

"They probably needed his help avoiding icebergs," Glory stated with a knowing nod. "A responsible job, to be sure. Did you notice how bumpy things were last night? Why, my liver just about jumped right out of me! I'm so glad things are calmer today."

Faith was glad to see things calmer, as well, and she hoped her relationship with Cal would mirror the smooth sailing conditions.

"And after the singles party," Glory continued, reading from the program again, "there's an Oriental cooking demonstration. That sounds interesting. What are you going to do this afternoon? They're also showing a movie in the theater."

Faith had no intention of being cooped up in a dark theater or the Showboat Lounge while there was beautiful scenery to be photographed. They'd left the open ocean and were cruising Yakutat Bay on their way to Hubbard Glacier. Faith was looking forward to getting some telephoto shots of the seals she'd seen through her binoculars earlier. There was plenty of wildlife to view in this bay and Faith wanted to make the most of her opportunities. Glancing at her watch, Faith said, "You better hurry, Glory, or you'll be late for that singles champagne party."

"My heavens, you're right!" Glory leapt up as if springloaded. "I better go before all the good men are taken. I do hope Ivan will be there."

Glory had no sooner left than Faith was joined by the Kecks. "Howz by you?" Bud Keck asked Faith with a big smile.

"Fine," Faith replied. "And you both?"

"Fine," Nora Keck replied. "We stayed in our cabin all day yesterday, keeping each other warm, didn't we, honeybear? It's *soooo* cold here. Since we're from Miami, we're not used to all this snow and ice.''

"But we have our own way of heating things up, don't we, fruitcup?" Bud said with a wide grin.

Nora gave him a playful slap on the shoulder, jiggling the dangling bracelet of green apples she wore. "Now, honeybear, you behave yourself."

There was no mistaking the love these two shared. As Faith left them together, she couldn't help wondering if she and Nigel would ever have a love like that, the kind that would last for decades. But when she tried to picture it, all she saw was Cal grinning at her from a rocking chair beside hers.

Faith spent a very productive and satisfying afternoon on the upper deck taking pictures. Because they were so far north, the sun was never directly overhead, therefore the light was filtered and softened while the shadows were rich in contrast. She'd already taken several rolls of film and it was only their third day out.

She'd also explored the ship, walking from stern to bow and was rather pleased with herself for knowing which was which. She'd even located the swimming pool on the sports deck, which actually had one brave and crazy fool swimming in it.

She hadn't seen Cal since that morning. She'd heard him return to the cabin while she was in the bathroom, getting dressed after her shower. He might have been absent earlier, but she hadn't forgotten him. How could she, with his things cluttering up the tiny bathroom. His shaving kit was the same one she'd bought for him as a get-well gift when he'd been in the hospital.

As for her, she was feeling pretty good. She was almost ready to go meet Ivan for their dinner date. Her hair was actually behaving and her dress fit her perfectly. It was a dream of sandwashed silk with a softly flaring skirt that caressed her legs as she walked. The tropical swirl of blue and green colors brought out the green in her eyes. A pair of filigree fiery opal drop earrings along with a matching necklace added just the right touch. Checking her reflection in the mirror, she added a smidge more lipstick—misty mauve—before nodding approvingly. Perfect.

Thinking she looked pretty damn good, Faith opened the bathroom door and stepped into the cabin, only to have Cal glare at her and say, "Where do you think you're going dressed like that?"

Five

―――

Faith stared at Cal in disbelief. "I beg your pardon?"

"You heard me."

"I couldn't possibly have heard you *correctly,* however."

"I asked you where you think you're going dressed like—" Cal waved his hand at her dress "—that."

"Like what?" she asked in confusion, looking down at her outfit and seeing nothing wrong with it. "You're saying you don't like what I'm wearing?"

"It's not a matter of liking or not liking. That dress isn't...appropriate."

"Not appropriate?" Faith repeated in amazement. "For what?"

"For you."

In Faith's opinion, Cal was digging himself deeper with every word. "And exactly what does that mean?" she inquired icily.

Cal realized his mistake, but it was too late to back down now. "Why don't you change into another dress?" he suggested with a coaxing smile. "That denim one in the closet is nice."

"I've been dressing myself for some time now, Cal. I really don't need a fashion advisor," she added disdainfully, reaching for her purse, which was already laid out on her bed. When she straightened, Cal was blocking her path to the cabin door.

"Where are you going?" he demanded with uncharacteristic interest.

"I'm going out."

"With who?"

"With *whom*," she corrected him. "And what makes you think I'm going out with someone?"

"Because a woman doesn't put on a dress like that to eat alone."

"I'm not even going to dignify that with an answer. If I thought you really meant it, I'd—"

"Just answer me this," he interrupted her. "Are you meeting that officer in the monkey suit?"

She stared at him in bewilderment. "What officer in the monkey suit?"

"The one who had his arm around you last night at the cocktail party."

"Oh. You mean John? No, I'm not going out with him. Not tonight at least."

Cal eyed her disapprovingly. "I thought you were close to finding Mr. Right with that Nigel guy? What do you think he'd have to say if he knew you were seeing other men?"

"Nigel is very understanding."

"Sounds like a sap, to me."

"Nigel is not a sap! He's sweet and intelligent and dignified—everything you're not."

"Hey, his loss," Cal retorted with a wicked grin.

Faith glared at him. "Out of my way, Masters."

He ignored her order. "Not so fast. If you're not having dinner with that officer, who are you having dinner with?"

Faith didn't consider the answer to that question to be any of Cal's business and she was about to tell him so when she got the sudden image of him playing this protective role before. Throughout her college years, he'd always been there for her; riding his bike over to the library to accompany her home if she had to study late, covering for her when a prohibited hot plate she and Chris had smuggled into their dorm room had blown a fuse and sent the entire wing into darkness.

Keeping those memories in mind, Faith relented and said, "If you must know, I'm going out with Ivan."

"Ivan who?" Cal immediately demanded.

"I don't know his last name," she said in exasperation.

Cal looked shocked. "You're going out with some guy and you don't even know his last name?"

"Listen, you've gone out with plenty of women whose *first* name you barely knew, let alone their last name! So stop giving me a hard time. You probably left some brokenhearted woman back in Seattle, didn't you?"

"Nope."

"What about Bambi?" Faith asked, seeming to recall that that was the name of the last woman she'd heard him associated with.

"Barbi not Bambi," he corrected her. "And it was never serious between us."

It never was serious with Cal, Faith silently noted.

"Stop trying to change the subject. We were talking about you and this Ivan guy. Where did you meet him, anyway?" Seeing the telltale lifting of her chin that portended imminent danger, Cal hurriedly added, "I'm only asking because I'm your friend and I'm concerned, okay?"

Somewhat mollified, Faith replied, "I met him at the cocktail party last night. He is a perfect gentleman."

"Little guy, has a mustache, speaks with an accent?" Cal said.

"That's not how I'd describe him," Faith replied.

"I remember him now."

"Bully for you." Old college memories aside, Faith's irritation was getting the better of her. "Move it, Masters. You're in my way. I'm going to be late."

Cal reluctantly moved partly, but not completely, away. "I still think you should change into something—"

"More matronly," she inserted angrily. "Yes, I know. You made that very clear. However, I don't give a tinker's damn what you think," she said, so aggravated with him that she really didn't care what he thought. Here she'd felt great when she'd left the bathroom and he'd gone and ruined it.

Cal saw the pain flash across her expressive eyes. "Hey, kid," he said softly. "I'm just worried about you, that's all."

"Don't."

Her curt reply angered him. He'd tried to reach out to her and she'd slapped him down. Stepping away from the door completely, Cal made a sweeping gesture of mock invitation with his arm—ushering her on her way. "In that case, don't let me keep you."

"I won't."

"I'm sure we'll meet up again shortly. For drinks before dinner. You and Ivan. Me and Natasha."

That stopped Faith in her tracks. "Natasha? Who is Natasha?"

"She's tall, nicely stacked, has long black hair and she's a friend of Ivan's. Which will make it all very cozy, won't it?" Cal observed sarcastically. "She invited me out to dinner this evening."

"She seems the type who would," Faith muttered. Natasha wasn't the kind to wait around to be asked. She was the kind who wore black leather and no underwear.

Cal raised an eyebrow at her. "Meaning what?"

"Meaning that she's not the wallflower type."

"You got that right," Cal agreed.

To Faith, what was implied was that *she,* by comparison, *was* more the wallflower type. Well, Faith was tired of blending into the background. All the outfits she'd carefully chosen for this trip were meant to be knockouts. Not flagrantly eye-popping like Natasha's little leather number. No, Faith had opted for class and pizzazz instead.

The dress she was wearing now, the one Cal was objecting to so vehemently, had that combination of class and pizzazz. The sweetheart neckline displayed her creamy skin to full advantage including a bit of cleavage, but it was nothing compared to the plunging belly-button display of Natasha's last night.

Faith knew it was useless to compare herself to Natasha. It was the sure way to an ulcer. Natasha was tall, thin, slinky and drop-dead gorgeous. Everything Faith knew she wasn't. What's more, the other woman had the kind of perfect hair that would automatically make any normal woman want to strangle her.

The fact that Natasha was going out with Cal had nothing to do with Faith's feelings of jealousy and dismay, she told herself. She was jealous of the woman's perfect hair and slinky body; it was nothing more than that.

Still, Faith had several weapons in her own arsenal. She refused to be a victim of crushing self-doubt. She knew her own strengths, and a consultation with a beauty expert a few months ago had improved Faith's knowledge on how to make the most of what she had.

Tilting her head, she recalled that attitude she'd had in the ship's lounge, when she'd felt on top of the world. She needed some of that right now. The idea suddenly struck her that Cal might be reacting the way he was because she looked *too* good. It probably wasn't the truth, but it made her feel better. A half smile even curved her lips. "I hope you and Natasha have a very nice evening," she said politely.

"I'm sure we will," Cal said. "We'll meet you and Ivan in the Topside Lounge in ten minutes. Don't be late or I might have to come looking for you."

"Don't be ridiculous." Her earlier exasperation returned tenfold. "You're playing this protective-brother act way too strongly, Masters."

"You never used to complain before," he retorted.

"Yes, well, that was a long time ago. I've been on my own for years now. I've even been married. Trust me, I know how to take care of myself."

"Ycah, right."

"Unless you're frightened that Natasha is a man-eater and you're looking for a little protection yourself?" Faith countered with a mocking lift of her eyebrow.

"I can handle Natasha."

Faith just bet he could, and she refused to think about him *handling* Natasha. The image threatened to ruin her appetite.

Faith thought she couldn't get any more annoyed with Cal, but an hour later she found that wasn't true. The display he and Natasha were putting on across the table from them in the ship's lounge was shameless and it made Faith want to grab something sharp to pry them apart. Like a can opener, maybe. The two of them were closer than sardines in a packed can. What's more, Cal didn't even have the decency to fight off Natasha's boldly flirtatious advances. It was enough to make Faith's blood burn.

"American men are so charming," Natasha purred.

"You think so?" Faith said. "Personally, I find continental men much more charming."

"Of course men from my country are famous for charm," Ivan inserted.

"And what country is that?" Cal immediately inquired.

"He can't talk about it," Faith replied on Ivan's behalf. "It upsets him too much."

Ivan nodded and looked suitably sorrowful.

"You and Natasha come from the same country, then?" Cal asked.

"Yes," Natasha confirmed. "Although Ivan is from north and I am from south. South is much warmer. Peoples are much warmer."

"You get any warmer and you'll set off the smoke detectors," Faith muttered under her breath as Natasha draped herself against Cal's side.

"What was that, Faith?" Cal inquired with a devilish twinkle in his blue eyes.

"I said, I can see how . . . *friendly* Natasha is," Faith observed cryptically.

"Cal told me that you are friends with him," Natasha stated with a sultry smile. "Buddies, he said. Is American term, yes? Means friend? Is nice that he thinks of you as buddy. You are . . . how do you say? You are 'one of the boys.'"

With one look, Natasha relegated Faith to the pile of zero-sex-appeal items such as diapers, dirty socks and ratty old slippers.

"Cal and I go way back," Faith said. "You could say that I've had to save his hide more than one time."

"As I've saved yours," Cal returned. Then, turning to Natasha, he said, "When we were in college, Faith made the mistake of stepping on a nail and I gallantly came to her rescue, carrying her to the nearest clinic."

Natasha blinked at him adoringly. "Was heroic thing to do."

"He didn't carry me," Faith denied, remembering the incident very well. "He put his arm around me while I hopped on one foot the block and a half to the campus clinic."

"I would have carried her if she hadn't had a fit about me picking her up," Cal said.

"You were moaning and groaning when you picked me up," Faith retorted.

"I was just kidding you," Cal maintained.

"I wasn't amused," Faith snapped.

"I think is time we went to dinner now," Ivan inserted. "I have something special planned."

"I have something special planned also," Natasha informed Cal seductively.

I can just imagine what that is, Faith thought to herself. Faith had run into a few "men's women" before, women who wouldn't give anyone of their own gender the time of day, but she'd never met one who suffered from the affliction as intensely as Natasha.

It was just her luck that although Cal and Natasha were seated halfway across the dining room, they were still directly in Faith's line of vision. The sight of Natasha hand-feeding Cal was enough to make Faith feel like gagging.

"You are not eating," Ivan noted in concern. "You are perhaps feeling ocean-ill?"

"Seasick? No, I'm fine. That's not it."

"You are having some other problem? I am good listener," Ivan assured her. "You can speak to me. About anything. Perhaps you did something you now regret . . ." He trailed off meaningfully.

"I regret *not* doing something," Faith muttered. "Like hitting Cal when I had the chance."

Ivan was disappointed with her answer. "That is all?"

"Boiling him in oil sounds good, too."

"Forget Cal. Eat your dinner. Unless food is not to your liking?"

Ivan had ordered for both of them, but the truth was that Faith wasn't that fond of crab's legs. It reminded her of an episode from her college days, when Cal had felt so sorry for a small tankful of live crabs at a local restaurant that he'd bought them all and driven all the way to the sound to set them free. It was one of those impulsive, unpredictable things he was apt to do. And it had made her fall for him even harder. Luckily, she no longer wore those rose-colored glasses. With her contacts in place, she could see just fine. And what she saw going on between Natasha and Cal didn't please her one bit!

"Is not right for such lovely woman to be so sad," Ivan said.

"I'm sorry. And I'm not sad, just irritated. Even so, I'm not turning out to be a very good dinner companion, am I?" Faith resolutely turned away so that Cal and Natasha were no longer in her line of vision. Smiling at Ivan, she said, "So tell me, how are you enjoying the cruise so far? Did you see the seals out on the ice floes this afternoon? The scenery so far has certainly been beautiful, hasn't it?"

"You are beautiful," Ivan returned. "Your beauty is lasting. Natasha has sex appeal now, but will not have in few more years. Things are already sagging. You are much better woman than Natasha. Any man with eyes can see. You have true beauty. Like a Madonna. Not rock singer, you understand," he hurriedly assured her.

No, Faith thought to herself. Natasha was the one who dressed more like Madonna.

"You are like painting I saw in book once. Was painting by Renoir. Woman had wonderful skin. She had glow."

"Why, thank you, Ivan. That's very kind of you to say. I've seen some of the portraits done by Renoir. I was in Chicago for a conference a few years back and visited the Art Institute there. The Impressionists are among my favorites," Faith confessed.

"Mine, as well," Ivan declared.

That got them talking about art and to her delight she found that Ivan was extremely knowledgeable on the subject. From the Impressionists they moved on to English watercolor artists like Turner.

"I have etchings by Turner of sea and boats," Ivan said. "Found them in small gallery in Anchorage. They are in my cabin. But no, would not be proper to have you come to cabin."

At that moment, Faith happened to look up in time to see Natasha nuzzling Cal's ear. In light of *their* uninhibited behavior, going to Ivan's cabin didn't seem improper. Faith hadn't lied when she'd assured Cal earlier that she knew how to take care of herself. Besides, Faith had a feeling that after what she'd already been through that evening, handling Ivan would be no problem. "That would be fine," she said.

But when she got to his cabin, it wasn't fine. It was awkward at first, as Ivan couldn't immediately locate the

Turner etching and instead invited her to share the bottle of champagne he had chilling. Faith refused and was about to leave when Ivan suddenly lurched toward her. Faith leapt up from the studio couch on which they'd both been sitting, and the next thing she knew, Ivan had somehow ended up on the floor.

"My back!" he yelped.

Faith kept her distance at first, suspicious that this was just another ploy of his. But one look at Ivan's contorted features told her that he truly was in pain.

"I'm sorry," she said, cautiously kneeling beside him. "Did you hurt yourself badly? Would you like me to call a doctor?"

"No doctor," Ivan said. "Back has gone before. Is old war injury." He grimaced again. "I need hot water bottle from bathroom."

"Certainly." Faith filled the rubber bottle with hot water and returned to the cabin to find that Ivan had somehow dragged himself onto the other couch that had been turned down earlier by the purser into a bed. "I'm sorry about this. I feel badly, but you really shouldn't have grabbed at me like that." She handed him the hot water bottle. "You're sure you don't need a doctor?"

"No doctor," Ivan repeated.

"Well then . . . good night." Faith let herself out of the cabin, leaving Ivan alone on the bed muttering in a foreign language she couldn't understand.

When Faith walked into her own cabin a few minutes later, she found a very different scene going on. Another bed, only this time Cal was the one sprawled out on it while Natasha was leaning over him. It didn't take a rocket scientist to figure out what was going on.

"Excuse me for interrupting," Faith said icily.

Natasha quickly straightened up. "Not interrupting," she said. "He is not well."

"Cal's sick?" Faith asked in concern, hurrying over to join Natasha at his bedside. "What's wrong?"

"He drank too much. Made him sleepy."

That didn't sound like Cal. "Are you sure that's what happened? Maybe I should call a doctor?"

"No, he will be fine in morning. Drink was called Rocket. I told him was strong. He would not listen." With a careless shrug of her shoulders, Natasha said, *"Men."*

"Yeah, *men,*" Faith agreed. "I'll take care of Cal now, Natasha."

"He is lucky to have friend like you," Natasha said.

"He might not think so in the morning," Faith muttered as Natasha left.

Natasha returned to her cabin to find Ivan spread-eagled on the bed. "Did you get information from woman?"

Ivan groaned. "She put my back out."

"I do not want to hear details of your sexual activities, Ivan."

"Was not sexual activities. Was accident. I fell on floor and now back is out. Mission was not successful," Ivan muttered. "What about you? Did you get information from man?"

"No."

"Did you return to his cabin and search it as we planned?"

"Plan did not work. My mission was not successful, either."

"What do you mean?"

"I did what manual said. I slipped him a...mickey is American term, yes? But bar was dark. I could not see how much I was giving him."

"What did you do? Kill him?"

"Of course I did not kill him!" Natasha angrily denied. "I did not give him enough. He was not unconscious. Just very sleepy and groppy....groggy...something like that. I could not search cabin. He kept opening eyes and staring at me. And then woman burst in."

"How could you make such a mistake?" Ivan demanded.

"I am new at this job," Natasha retorted defensively. "Did not have special training like you. And even with special training, you did not do any better," she said. "You got no information from woman. I was not only one to fail. Fate is not being good to us."

"Do not mention curse again," Ivan warned her.

"I did not," she protested. "*You* did. Now what do we do?"

"Time to study manual again," Ivan declared with a sigh.

Faith watched over Cal's sleeping form with worried eyes. It wasn't like him to drink so much he practically passed out. She couldn't recall his ever doing anything like that before, even the time their football team had lost fifty-two to nothing and all the guys in the dorm had gotten gut-retchingly drunk. All but Cal.

Of course, she didn't know what he was like while he'd traveled as a news correspondent for *World News* magazine. Maybe he'd picked up the habit of drinking to excess while he'd been on the road. Although he never talked about it, Faith realized that a lot of the things Cal had covered in his reports were devastatingly tragic. He'd seen enough pain and despair in the course of his travels to drive most men to drink.

But, again, Cal wasn't most men. He was more infuriating than most, but also more dependable. You could depend on him to act a certain way. Where she was concerned, he always took great pleasure in teasing her. He'd never taken great pleasure in kissing her... until yesterday.

She wondered if he had taken as much pleasure in it as she had. And then she wondered if that's why he'd gotten so drunk. Because of their kiss. Was he afraid she was going to turn into a clinging vine he wouldn't be able to get rid of? Pain pierced her heart, like a rose thorn pricking her skin.

So far, Chris's predictions about Faith's getting over Cal by being in such close quarters with him hadn't been accurate. Oh, she'd gotten angry with him, furious even. But like a stubborn thorn, she couldn't seem to dislodge him from her heart. She didn't appreciate the fact that he'd stolen his way back in after all these years. She'd accepted reality and made a life for herself. A life she was very happy with.

She was not happy, however, with the return of this . . . infatuation, for want of a better word. It was more suited to a twenty-year-old. She was in her thirties now. Older, definitely. A little wiser. Supposedly more experienced. So what had happened here? Where had her plans to get over Cal gone awry?

Looking at him lying there so still, she was reminded of seeing him lying in the hospital in Seattle after he'd collapsed. It was so rare to see Cal motionless. Even when he was being lazy, he vibrated with life and mischief.

Reaching out, Faith tenderly smoothed a lock of his brown hair from his forehead before catching herself and testing his forehead in a practical way to see if he was running a fever. Checking her medicine case, she found a thermometer strip—the kind that pressed onto the forehead.

The incongruous sight of Cal with a thermometer strip pressed to his forehead made her smile, if only slightly. This was the only way she could get away with checking his temperature, when he was practically unconscious. To say he'd never been a good patient was an understatement.

To her relief, Cal's temperature was normal. Hers, on the other hand, felt as if it were rising as her proximity to Cal started taking its toll on her. Chastising herself for reacting like a teenager, Faith moved to the safer turf of her own twin bed and busied herself by taking off her opal jewelry and carefully putting it away in her travel bag. Legend had it that opals were able to absorb the emotions of its wearer. If so, she pitied the poor stones, for they'd picked up a truckload of emotions tonight, all of them conflicting. Affection, anger, yearning, desire, concern—all for Cal.

He mumbled something in his sleep. She told herself he was all right, that there was nothing to worry about. But when he mumbled again half an hour later, she rushed over to his bed. She hadn't changed into her pajamas yet, just in case she should need to call the doctor for him. Besides, she was too restless, too worried to sleep.

"Cal?" she whispered softly, sitting on the bed beside him. She was leaning over him to check his temperature again with the palm of her hand when Cal suddenly grabbed hold of her supporting arm and tumbled her into bed with him.

Blinking at her sleepily, he proceeded to kiss her. Deeply. Sensuously.

Once again, Faith was caught unaware. Unprepared for the rush of desire. She tried to murmur a halfhearted protest, but the sound was merely incorporated into their kiss. By parting her lips, she'd made it possible for him to add a seductive swipe of his tongue to his repertory of temptation. He then improvised by wickedly nibbling on the sweet softness of her lower lip.

Faith blindly responded, done in by her own attraction to him. She greeted his tongue with her own, mimicking his actions nibble for nibble as well as doing some creative exploring of her own. Sandwiched as she was between the mattress beneath her and Cal's muscular body above her, she didn't have much room for maneuvering, but she managed to slide her arms around his neck and guide her fingers into his dark hair.

His hands were also busy, stroking her from shoulder to hip. The sandwashed silk of her dress was a powerful amplifier, magnifying the magic of his caresses. He gave her teasing hints as to the final destination of his touch, moving his hands around her waist and up her rib cage to temptingly cup her breast.

Faith gasped with pleasure as Cal huskily murmured his appreciation of her feminine curves. She almost jumped out of her skin when he gently rubbed his thumb over her silk-covered nipple. She couldn't think. She didn't care. She wanted this. Wanted him.

His mouth continued to move over hers as if he were fascinated with and addicted to the shape and taste of it. One kiss blended into the next, each more heady and passionate than the last. Wrapped in a cocoon of exhilarating bliss, Faith returned his caresses measure for measure.

Eventually, his kisses wandered from her parted lips to her throat before lowering to the pale curves just visible above the neckline of her dress. He tempted her with evocative nibbles and the stealthy seduction of his fingers. It wasn't until she felt a draft of cool air hitting her bare back that she realized he'd undone the zipper on her dress. The neckline now gaped, allowing his lips further access into unexplored territory.

She arched against him as he lightly teased the rosy crests of her breasts with his open mouth. The thin silk of her bra provided no protection at all and in fact added to her pleasure as he blew against the material he'd just moistened. Faith shivered with unconcealed delight as he shifted her body so that she rested more intimately against him.

Nudging his knee between her legs, he found a place for himself there. She could feel his arousal. Strong. Hard. Throbbing. He wanted her. There was no denying that. No hiding it.

She melted against him, a victim of the hungry ache prowling deep within her. Pleasure replaced coherent thought and it wasn't until Cal had Faith halfway out of her dress that she realized exactly where this was leading.

Faith knew she should stop this, but she wanted Cal so much that she couldn't resist the temptation of being in his arms. It was sheer heaven. Until Cal murmured, "Natasha..."

Six

Faith froze. *Natasha? Natasha!* Faith felt as if she'd just been doused with ice water. With one word, heaven had become hell.

She shoved Cal away from her with such force that she almost knocked him clear off the narrow bed. Leaping to her feet, she hurriedly tugged her loose dress back on.

"What's the matter?" Cal demanded, wide-awake now, although still a little bleary-eyed.

"I am *not* Natasha!" Faith shouted.

"I never said you were," he denied, grabbing his head and wincing at the decibel level of her voice. "Wait a second. Faith! It was a mistake. Come back here...."

But Faith had already gone into the bathroom, slamming the door for good measure.

Gripping the sink with both hands, Faith bit the inside of her cheek to prevent herself from crying. The bathroom walls were paper-thin and Cal was right outside. She didn't want him hearing her sob like a heartbroken idiot, even though that's exactly how she felt.

Humiliation burned its way to her heart, leaving a path of ashes in its wake. A mistake. *She* was a mistake. He'd actually said so. She closed her eyes, as if by doing so she could blot out the past fifteen minutes of her life.

Cal had done it to her again. Made an idiot of her. Anger rose within her, helping to anesthetize some of her pain. She wasn't sure which emotion—humiliation or rage—caused her hands to shake as she stripped off her silk dress and yanked on the pair of jeans and sweatshirt she'd left lying in the bathroom this morning. She also wasn't sure who she was angrier at—Cal for thinking she was Natasha, or herself for letting him kiss her in the first place.

She was doing a great job of getting over Cal all right, Faith sarcastically berated herself. What did he have to do for her to get the message? He wasn't interested in her as anything other than a friend.

She needed to get away from him. Pulling open the bathroom door, she vowed that if Cal tried to block her way out of the cabin, she'd mow him down.

He was sitting on the edge of the bed, eyeing her warily. "Faith..."

She ignored him, heading straight for the cabin door.

"If you'd just calm down a minute..." he continued. "Hey! Where are you going?"

She left without answering verbally, although the way she slammed the door told him plenty.

It took Cal over an hour, but he finally tracked Faith down to one of the upper decks. He'd already searched both lounges, the casino, the library, the theatre and every nook and cranny in between. He found her stashed in an out-of-the-way corner, sitting in a deck chair—broodingly watching the sunset, which was still coloring the sky even though it was nearing midnight.

Having had to search half the ship, Cal was not amused with her. He wasn't real pleased with himself, either. How could he hope to explain things to Faith when he wasn't clear about anything himself? He *hadn't* thought she was

Natasha. But how did he explain that he hadn't been thinking clearly when he'd kissed her? How could he admit that he wasn't sure how he'd ended up with Faith in his arms when the last thing he remembered was Natasha helping him back to the cabin; hence, his use of Natasha's name.

It sounded like a muddled explanation, even to him. And that's exactly how he felt. Muddled. The cold, outside air and three cups of strong black coffee had only helped clear his mind a little, making him wonder what the hell was in that drink he'd had. He'd drunk half a bottle of ouzo once, and even that hadn't left him feeling this out of it.

Cal didn't know what had come over him. Kissing her once had been reprehensible enough on his part, but this was the second time it had happened in as many days. What was even worse, a part of him wanted it to happen again. Luckily, the nobler, wiser, saner part of him knew better.

The truth was that Cal was torn between his feelings for Faith—wanting to make love with her and wanting to protect her from himself. This was definitely a first for him, and it wasn't a situation that pleased him one iota. He suspected his own expression was just as brooding as hers as he dropped into the chair nearest hers.

Faith studiously ignored him, not easy to do since the air was thick enough to cut with a knife. Sexual tension still resonated between them as the aftereffect of their recent intimate embrace. At least it resonated from her. She had no idea what Cal was thinking, and his face gave her no indication of his thoughts—aside from the fact that they weren't pleasant ones.

"We seem to have a problem here," he said in a gritty voice. "This isn't working."

"It certainly isn't," Faith immediately confirmed.

"I know we said before we'd try to stay out of each other's hair..." Cal trailed off, remembering with vivid clarity the silky softness of Faith's hair as he'd held her in his arms a short while ago. "Listen, I'll stay out of your way as much as humanly possible for the remainder of the cruise."

"Fine."

"Good," he repeated. "You can go back to the cabin now. You don't have to sit up here freezing to death. I won't bother you again."

"Yeah, right," she muttered without thinking. She was beginning to doubt the day would ever come when Cal didn't bother her.

Misinterpreting her words, Cal stiffened. "Are you saying you don't trust me?"

Faith made no reply. In some ways, she'd trust Cal with her life. In others, she didn't trust him any more than she trusted herself.

"Don't be an idiot," he said curtly. "You can trust me. But to make you feel better, you can have the cabin to yourself tonight."

He was gone before she could say a word.

Faith kept her eyes on the sunset, refusing to let any more tears fall. Her vision was momentarily blurred but she blinked back the telltale moisture.

She *was* an idiot, just as Cal had said. She kept secretly hoping things would change but they never did. And they never would. Cal was never going to love her the way a man loves a woman. He had to be furious or completely out of it before he would kiss her . . . and even then, he thought he was kissing someone else. Someone more his type. Someone who wasn't a buddy. Someone like Natasha. Faith couldn't believe she'd made herself so vulnerable again.

Only this time, it was worse. Because, unlike that disastrous New Year's Eve kiss so long ago, this time she'd had a taste of the forbidden fruit and found it addictive. Cal had kissed her, seduced her with his tongue, tempted her with his caresses. But only because he'd thought I was Natasha, she fiercely reminded herself.

"Damn, damn, damn," she muttered, hitting her clenched fist on the deck chair's armrest as the tears started to slowly fall, threatening to dislodge her contacts.

God, she was tired of this pain. She didn't want to feel this way about Cal anymore. It simply hurt too much.

It wasn't the first time Cal had spent the night in a chair and he doubted it would be the last. As chairs went, this one in the ship's open library area wasn't that bad. The resulting crick in his neck wasn't as bad as it could have been, either.

Cal had developed the ability to fall asleep regardless of the discomfort of his surroundings that first year he'd been on the road for *World News* magazine. Through the years, from the back streets of Belfast to the U.S. Marines landing in Somalia, he'd learned to grab a few z's wherever he could—on a plane, bus, even on the back of a camel once. That episode had almost ended up with him breaking his neck, Cal recalled, let alone getting a crick in it.

Compared to what he'd lived through in the past, this chair was plush accommodation indeed. Not that he planned on spending the rest of the cruise sleeping in it. He hoped Faith would have calmed down by this morning, although he wasn't fooling himself into thinking she'd forgiven him or that she was ready to kiss and make up.

The phrase made Cal sigh. He didn't know what had happened to him last night. That drink must have packed a hell of a wallop for one or two glasses to put him out like that. While some of his impressions were hazy, he remembered holding Faith *very* clearly. Remembered every intimate detail of her lush body. Memorized the feel of her mouth melting under his.

Raking one hand through his hair, Cal swore softly. He didn't know what was happening to him. But somehow, some way, his impressions of Faith had shifted. Shifted, hell—they'd taken a 360-degree turn. From affection to lust. What was wrong with him?

It wasn't as if he'd ever been the romantic type. His parent's bitter divorce when he was thirteen had taken care of that. Twenty years later, his parents still weren't speaking, their hatred of each other as intense as ever. Having seen firsthand the devastating havoc the unholy state of matrimony could wreak, Cal had no desire to ever get married himself. But he did appear to suddenly have a strong desire for Faith.

As his name suggested, Cal Masters was used to being the master of his own fate. He enjoyed being footloose and fancy-free. At least, he always had in the past...

Shaking his head as if to rid himself of those kinds of disturbing thoughts, Cal groaned at the resultant jackhammer battering at his temple. A more cautious look at his watch told him that it was almost six a.m. Time for some aspirin and coffee. A lot of it. A couple gallons of it. Maybe then he'd be able to make some sense out of this mess.

Faith was awake to see the sunrise at 4:33. Which meant she'd gotten a grand total of four hours' sleep. As promised, Cal hadn't come back to the cabin last night. Chances were, he'd gone to find Natasha.

It was now almost six in the morning and, like a phoenix rising from the ashes, Faith had reached a decision in the darkest hour of the brief yet endless night that had just passed. If Cal was so stupid that he couldn't tell the gold, meaning her, from the dross, meaning Natasha, then he deserved what he got. It was his loss. She wasn't going to agonize over it.

She'd wasted enough time. She'd looked back long enough. It was time to look forward, toward the future— her future. With Nigel? That, she didn't know. But she did know that she would make it through this and come out the other side. She was battered but definitely not beaten.

Counting today, there were still five days left on this cruise and she wasn't going to waste another one of them brooding over Cal. Time to get out and enjoy herself. Time to put the past behind her.

Also time to get off the ship, for this morning was the first stop since they'd boarded in Whittier. Today's destination was Skagway, and Faith had signed up for a bus tour of part of the Yukon Territory. She'd signed up on her own, and that's how she planned on spending her day. On her own. Rediscovering herself and staying clear of Cal.

Ten minutes later, she was dressed and out of the cabin, after having first called the purser to complain about the shower head, which had ceased working in the middle of her shower. Luckily, she'd already rinsed the shampoo from her hair or she would really have been in trouble.

She'd left a note for Cal saying she wouldn't be back to the cabin until six that night. Along with her jeans and ankle boots, Faith wore an oversize bulky red sweater with one of her favorite marcasite pins, a half-moon made for wishing. At the last minute, she decided to add her blue denim down vest on top of her sweater.

Breakfast was alfresco, melon and two pieces of toast from the outdoor buffet at the front of the ship. Her choice. There was a veritable banquet of food offered. She just wasn't hungry. Normally, people gained weight from eating all the good food on a cruise. At this rate, she'd be losing weight. Maybe she'd fit into a size twelve after all, she encouraged herself.

By the time they were preparing to dock, Faith was one of the first in line, her camera at the ready. She'd already taken some shots. As they were waiting for the gangplank to be lowered, the ship's cruise director gave a brief orientation over the intercom system. "Those painted rocks on the cliff across from the ship aren't covered with graffiti. Those paintings include Skagway's Ship's Registry. The name of every ship that has docked here is on those rocks, along with the date of the ship's maiden cruise."

Faith felt as if *she* were embarking on a maiden cruise of her own—into unfamiliar waters. She wasn't sure if she and Cal would be able to remain friends after what had happened last night. She didn't think there was any going back this time. Which meant that she was traveling into uncharted territory ahead.

Her thoughts were interrupted by the unique sound of Glory's "Yoo-hoo, Faith! Have you seen Ivan this morning?'' Glory asked Faith the moment she and Rhoda had joined her near the head of the line.

Given her own problems, Faith had forgotten all about Ivan. "No, I haven't. Why? Were you supposed to meet him?" Faith wondered if Ivan's back had gotten worse. Perhaps she should have called a doctor for him, after all.

"No, I wasn't supposed to meet him. Not exactly. That is, we didn't have anything definite set up," Glory replied. "I was just wondering if you'd seen him yet this morning. Did you have plans for today?"

"Yes. I'm taking that bus tour of the Yukon Territory. But it doesn't leave for another hour and a half, so I thought I'd do some exploring in Skagway first."

"Sounds like a wonderful idea. Rhoda and I have signed up for that bus tour, too, haven't we, Rhoda?" Glory's friend made no reply. Not that Glory gave her any time to respond before barreling on to the next subject. "Where's Calvin this morning?"

"I have no idea," Faith replied.

"Isn't he joining you?"

"No."

"You've had another fight again, haven't you?" Glory said. "You know, for two people who are supposed to be friends, you two sure argue a lot. Reminds me of my Ralph. We used to fight like cats and dogs. Ever since we met back in kindergarten. I ended up being married to him for forty years, bless his soul. Maybe that will be the case with you and Calvin. As my daddy used to say, 'No person ever injured his eyesight by looking on the bright side.' So don't give up. There now—" Glory patted Faith's hand "—I can see it upsets you to talk about this right now, so we won't discuss it any more for the present. You can tell me all the details later. Meanwhile, I'll read to you from my guidebook, shall I? I've been studying up, you know. They're running a contest to see who can get the most answers right about Alaska and they're offering a prize to the one who wins. I've got the contest in the bag," Glory told Faith. "Ask me anything about Alaska. Go ahead, ask me."

"That's okay...." Faith said.

"The U.S. purchased Alaska from Russia in 1867 for 7.2 million," Glory proudly stated. "That works out to about two cents an acre! Not that I checked the math on that myself, you understand. That's what the guidebook said. I already got that answer right yesterday. Ask me another question."

"Look, they've got the gangplank down," Faith said, hoping to distract her. It didn't work.

"That's nice. Did you know that Alaska is derived from the Aleut Indian word *Alashka* meaning great land or mainland? That was Sunday's question. Aced that one, too."

"Good for you."

"Today's question is going to be about Skagway, I just know it. That's why I've been reading up." Glory opened her trusty guidebook to a page marked with a hunk bookmark. "Listen to this, it says here that in all Alaska there is no town to match the pioneer flavor of Skagway. The town sprang up overnight when gold was discovered in the Canadian Yukon in 1896. A year later, according to a Canadian Mounted Police report 'Skagway was little better than a hell on earth.' Gold. 1896. Little better than hell," Glory repeated to herself. "Okay, I've got that."

"Does it say anything in your guidebook about the story of Soapy Smith?" Faith asked, following that old maxim that if you can't beat 'em, join 'em. Besides, she'd always had a soft spot for Western tales.

"I'm not sure..." Glory frantically thumbed through the pages.

"Soapy Smith was supposedly Alaska's most notorious outlaw," Faith said, having done some reading of her own. "He created all kinds of scams to rob prospectors of their money. One of his most famous scams was to meet the people at the docks and collect five dollars from them to send a telegram to their families back East to let them know they'd arrived okay."

"That doesn't sound so bad. What was wrong? Was he charging too much?"

"You could say that, considering the fact that there were no telegraph wires out of Skagway at the time," Faith replied with a slight grin.

"Oh, my."

"Soapy ended up dying in a gunfight with another man, Frank Reid, who also died in the shootout and was declared a hero."

"Those were certainly violent times," Glory said grimly.

"It's my understanding that the Canadian gold-rush towns experienced far less crime and disorder, thanks to the Mounted Police." It was an angle that Faith thought deserved further attention, so she'd made a note of it as a possible story idea for the magazine. Being a good editor meant coming up with fresh story ideas and then matchmaking them with talented writers. Being a great editor meant doing it better than anyone else. Faith was a great editor. Unlike so many other things in her life right now, of that she was certain.

"Careful, Glory, you don't want to trip over the gangplank here...." Faith took the older woman's arm. Once they were on land, it took a moment or two for Faith to regain her land legs as she had to adjust to walking on solid ground instead of the deck of a pitching ship.

Glory appeared to also need a few moments to adapt. "Thank you, dear. It feels strange being back on terra firma after having gotten our sea legs, doesn't it? I suppose I'd better wait to read the rest of my guidebook for later."

The ever-quiet Rhoda tagged along beside them as they walked the short distance from the dock to Skagway's main street of Broadway. Faith stopped several times along the way to take pictures of the surrounding mountains cradling the small town. The sun was shining today, and the light reflected off the snowcapped peaks with such force that Faith was forced to put on her sunglasses. The Bette Davis, confidence-building sunglasses. She hoped they would still provide a morale boost as well as protection from glare.

She left Glory and Rhoda in a souvenir shop that proudly claimed it was the oldest gift shop in Alaska. Exploring on her own for a bit, Faith enjoyed the freedom of being alone. She took several pictures of the Arctic Brotherhood Hall, a strange building covered in driftwood. She got a particularly good shot of the sun hitting the wood directly over the front door, with the year 1899 displayed in weathered driftwood.

In fact, most of the false-front buildings and old stores along the street seemed to be a bit weathered, in keeping with the town's history, no doubt. Even the original wooden-plank sidewalks appeared to be carefully maintained. Horse-drawn carriages plying cruise-ship visitors to and fro added to the Wild West atmosphere.

"Faith, howz by you?" Bud Keck boomed as he and his wife caught sight of Faith. "Have you seen the cribs yet? You know, those little movable houses on wheels where the ladies practiced the oldest profession."

"I did see them, Bud," Faith replied. She'd even taken a picture of one of the more colorful ones, which had been turned into a gift shop. Above the door were the words "House of Negotiable Affection." The phrase had made Faith smile, really smile, for the first time that day.

"We saw Glory earlier and she said you're going on the bus tour to the Yukon. So are we, my honeybear and me," Nora informed her with a smile, tugging down the pineapple sweatshirt she wore over her Bermuda shorts. Her earrings were also pineapple-shaped. "Sounds like everyone has signed up for that bus tour."

"I certainly hope not," Faith muttered, thinking of Cal. She hadn't seen him at all yet today and she was in no hurry to do so.

But to her dismay, he was already sitting on the bus when she got on board. "Look, dear, there's Calvin," Glory announced.

Faith deliberately took the empty seat in front of rather than beside him. "I wouldn't have thought this tour would be his cup of tea," Faith said to Glory, referring to Cal in the third person. "I would have thought he'd be on that helicopter flight out over the glaciers," she added.

"Tell her I've been on enough helicopters to last me a lifetime," Cal told Glory.

Whereupon Glory dutifully said, "He's been on enough helicopters—"

"I heard him the first time," Faith said, saving Glory the chore of repeating Cal's words.

"You two aren't speaking to each other, huh?" Glory noted, looking from Cal's who-me? expression to Faith's cool look of disinterest. "Gee, that must have been some argument."

Grumbles from the line forming behind her forced Glory to quickly pick a seat. She chose the one next to Cal, leaving Rhoda to sit next to Faith.

As the bus tour began, Faith only heard one sentence out of ten from the bus driver-tour guide's spiel. Of all the luck. There had been six other optional tours out of Skagway offered by the ship's tour office. Who would have thought that Cal would end up on hers? But then, who would have thought that Chris would break her leg and that Cal would end up rooming with her in the first place, driving her crazy.

This was her first test since she'd made her resolution to get on with her life. She needed to look at Cal's presence that way. As a test. One she would ace, to use Glory's phrase.

She did so by simply pretending Cal wasn't there. There was plenty of rugged scenery on which to focus her attention and her telephoto lens. Cal was invisible to her.

"So, Calvin, you enjoying the tour so far?" Glory asked as their bus climbed up the summer-only road over the White Pass.

NO RISK, NO OBLIGATION TO BUY ... NOW OR EVER!

CASINO JUBILEE
"Scratch'n Match" Game

Here's how to play:

1. Peel off label from front cover. Place it in space provided at right. With a coin, carefully scratch off the silver box. Then check the claim chart to see what we have for you – FREE BOOKS and a gift – ALL YOURS! ALL FREE!

2. Send back this card and you'll receive brand-new Silhouette Desire® novels. These books have a cover price of $2.99 each, but they are yours to keep absolutely free.

3. There's no catch. You're under no obligation to buy anything. We charge nothing – ZERO – for your first shipment. And you don't have to make any minimum number of purchases – not even one!

4. The fact is thousands of readers enjoy receiving books by mail from the Silhouette Reader Service™ months before they're available in stores. They like the convenience of home delivery and they love our discount prices!

5. We hope that after receiving your free books you'll want to remain a subscriber. But the choice is yours – to continue or cancel, anytime at all! So why not take us up on our invitation, with no risk of any kind. You'll be glad you did!

YOURS FREE!

This lovely Victorian pewter-finish miniature is perfect for displaying a treasured photograph – and it's yours absolutely free – when you accept our no-risk offer.

© 1991 HARLEQUIN ENTERPRISES LIMITED

CASINO JUBILEE
"Scratch'n Match" Game

SCRATCH HERE

PLACE LABEL HERE

?

CHECK CLAIM CHART BELOW FOR YOUR FREE GIFTS!

YES! I have placed my label from the front cover in the space provided above and scratched off the silver box. Please send me all the gifts for which I qualify. I understand that I am under no obligation to purchase any books, as explained on the back and on the opposite page.

225 CIS ANE9 (U-SIL-D-03/94)

Name _____

Address _____ Apt. _____

City _____ State _____ Zip _____

CASINO JUBILEE CLAIM CHART	
🍒🍒🍒 / 🍒🍒🔔 / 🔔🔔🍒	WORTH 4 FREE BOOKS AND A FREE VICTORIAN PICTURE FRAME
	WORTH 4 FREE BOOKS
	WORTH 3 FREE BOOKS

CLAIM N° 1528

Offer limited to one per household and not valid to current Silhouette Desire® subscribers. All orders subject to approval.

DETACH AND MAIL CARD TODAY! ▼

Cal gave a noncommittal grunt, thankful that his mirrored sunglasses prevented Glory from seeing his expression. The older woman was like a bulldog, refusing to let him sit there in peace. Looking out the window, Cal likened the surrounding snow-covered landscape to the equally chilly vibes coming from Faith as she sat in the seat ahead of him.

He hadn't known she'd be on this tour, although it was the logical one for her to choose, given her affection for Westerns. The Gold Rush of '97 was one of the last Old West legends. It stood to reason she'd want to follow the path some of those prospectors had taken.

Up until this point, he'd made good on his promise to stay out of her way. But he missed her. Missed their verbal battles. Missed her in old ways... and new.

He'd gotten used to having her around, although he hadn't gotten used to this unsettling hunger in the pit of his stomach—a hunger for the taste of her. He wasn't the right man for her. He knew that. It didn't stop him from wanting her, though.

But it did stop him from acting on that desire. As for Faith's feelings toward him, well... she'd made it pretty clear she no longer trusted him. And that ate at him. Even though he wasn't sure he really trusted himself, either. Because where Faith was concerned, he no longer knew which end was up.

Cal didn't even notice the bus had stopped until he realized he was the only one still on board. Everyone else had rushed outside for a photo opportunity and to look over the historic marker for the Klondike Gold Rush.

Cal was slow to join the rest of the passengers. "There you are, Calvin. I wondered if you'd fallen asleep behind those glasses of yours," Glory stated. "Glad you decided to join us. You won't believe what those prospectors went through. Our guide was just telling us that over on the Chilkoot Trail they say that if a climber had to step out of line, he would freeze to death before someone would stop long enough to let him back in."

Cal felt as if he could freeze to death from the iciness emanating from Faith. She was smiling and joking with the Kecks, but when she looked at him, her smile disappeared and the frost came out. Come to think of it, she didn't even look *at* him as much as clear through him. He didn't like it. He was damn tempted to grab a handful of snow and toss a snowball at her. Or to grab her and kiss her until she melted.

Neither course of action was politically correct, Cal knew that. Not that he paid any attention to correctness, political or otherwise, as he leaned over the waist-high pile of snow at the side of the road and packed a handful of the cold stuff in his bare hands. He kept his back to Faith, so she wouldn't see what he was doing.

Pow! A snowball hit him dead center in the middle of his back, splattering against his thick wool sweater and trickling through the weave.

He turned around in time to see Faith hurrying into the bus, but only after having first given him a triumphant and utterly superior look. The little devil!

"I'll get you for that," Cal murmured as he walked past Faith's seat.

At Rhoda's startled look, Cal hastily clarified, "I was talking to Faith."

Faith ignored him.

Cal was disappointed. Somehow, he'd thought that her action meant she'd forgiven him. That they could still try to be pals. But she remained as distant as ever. He resumed his seat, his mood worse than when he'd left it.

Their next stop was no better as Faith continued her Ice Queen routine, devoting all her attention to her camera. Stung, Cal responded in kind, ignoring her twice as much as she was ignoring him. Aggravated, he returned to the bus.

"I just want to remind you folks of some safety rules," their bus driver was saying over the intercom system. "Now the rules state that if a bear chases you, you don't run and you certainly don't run toward this bus. Because the company forbids my allowing anyone on board with a bear behind."

"Bare behind. That's a good one!" Glory said, sitting beside Cal and smacking her hand on the knee of her polyester pants. "Bare behind." She chortled again. "Didn't you get it, Calvin?" Glory asked, seeing that he wasn't sharing her amusement.

"I got it."

"Then why aren't you laughing?" Glory demanded.

"I'm not in a humorous mood at the moment," Cal retorted.

"Ah." Glory nodded sagely. Since Faith was still outside on top of the pass taking pictures, Glory took the opportunity to say, "It's because of that fight you and Faith had, isn't it? Now you know you can talk to me about it, Calvin. I'm the soul of discretion. I wouldn't tell a soul, except for Rhoda, of course. But, as you may have noticed, Rhoda doesn't say much. Still, you shouldn't think that she doesn't think deep thoughts, because she does. You know about still waters running deep, don't you. But I'm rambling. There now—" she patted his hand "—I'll be quiet. You were just about to tell me all about you and Faith."

"No, I wasn't," Cal calmly denied.

"Why not?" Glory inquired.

"Cause it's none of your business," Rhoda turned clear around in her seat to say.

Cal and Glory looked at her in surprise.

"Take it from this still body of water," Rhoda elaborated. "Some people never get interested in anything until it's none of their business."

"Well, I never," Glory huffed.

"Yes, you have," Rhoda boldly contradicted. "And you never blabbed about it to others, either. So give the poor man a break and leave him be. Besides, his name is Cal, not Calvin."

For once, Glory was speechless.

* * *

"Tour bus Cal and woman took was full," Natasha reported morosely. "I tried everything. Used sex appeal on driver. Still could not get on bus to Yukon tour."

"Is just as well," Ivan replied. "My back is not yet well. Would not be able to ride bus today."

"If we do not find diamonds, you and back will be much worse," Natasha stated ominously, irritated by his constant complaining.

"I am reading manual to decide on next step," Ivan assured her. "Do not interrupt me. How can I think when you always interrupt?"

"Does manual say what to do next?"

"Manual does not cover this exact case," Ivan had to admit.

"You said manual had idea for every case."

"I thought was so."

"Keep reading, Ivan. Keep reading until you find solution to this problem. Is big book. Must be there somewhere."

"Is big ship. Diamonds must be somewhere, too."

"Diamonds are in woman's cabin, I know it," Natasha said.

"Repairman is in woman's cabin, fixing broken shower," Ivan said.

"We will search cabin afterward. How long can repairman take?"

"On Nabassi, repairmen take a week, maybe more to fix shower," Ivan replied.

"This is not Nabassi," Natasha reminded him.

"So here should take one day."

"One day? We are doomed," Natasha declared dramatically.

"Are not doomed. Manual will suggest something. Do not despair," Ivan said. "We outsmarted those on Nabassi, we will outsmart here, as well."

* * *

"I used to have the legs for that," Nora Keck told Faith as they watched the historic Gay Nineties show being put on for their benefit.

"You still do, fruitcup. She's got the best-looking legs in Miami," Bud bragged. "She was Miss Citrus back in 19—"

"Now, honeybear, there's no need to list dates," Nora interrupted him.

Upon arriving at their final destination of Carcross in Canada, everyone had been herded from the bus into a warehouse where lunch was being served—family-style—on long wooden tables with red-checkered table cloths. The tables faced one another rather than the stage. Faith had made sure to sit at a different table than Cal chose, but even so, she ended up only a few feet away from him, her back to his.

At first, she'd kept her attention on the view out the windows to her right, where she could see blue water, lush pine forests and the purple hue of the base of the mountain, the top portion of which was covered with snow. But then the show had started in the middle of their lunch of beef stew, sourdough biscuits with apple crisp for dessert. Faith, like the others, watched the show while she ate. There were only three entertainers on stage, a piano player, a fiddler who was really very good and a singer dressed in Gay Nineties garb—a red boa around her neck and a full-length dress that fit her like a glove.

As Cal watched the woman singing, he found himself wondering what Faith would look like in a dress like that. She had the figure for it. Not slinky, but lush. And with her porcelain skin and old-fashioned ways, Faith certainly fit the role of a historical heroine.

In college, Faith had dared him to read one of the medieval romances she favored, and it hadn't been as bad as he'd expected, although he'd never told her that. He had, however, insisted on checking out a few more of her historical romances for himself, amazed at some of the lines guys got away with in the Middle Ages. A few of them still worked today, he recalled with a grin. But the face he saw in his mind's eye wasn't just any woman's, it was Faith's.

And that bothered him. A lot. He found it very disturbing that he wasn't the least bit attracted to Natasha or any other woman on the ship, except the one woman he wasn't supposed to be having sexual fantasies about—his cabin mate and old college buddy, Faith.

When exactly, he wondered in bewilderment, had she gone from being a buddy to being a woman? Oh, he'd known she was a woman before. Sort of. Only he hadn't really let it register. Now his awareness of her was definitely registering, clear off the Richter scale!

When a group of cancan dancers came on stage, kicking their heels and showing off their petticoats and garters, Cal imagined Faith in that attire, as well. Whatever he had, he had it bad.

Faith noticed Cal's undivided attention on the women on stage. He was either deep in thought or he was ogling the ladies. Knowing Cal, she put her money on the latter.

"Sorry I'm late," Faith breathlessly apologized to the bus driver. After the show, she'd gotten delayed waiting for a store owner to remove something from the window for her to purchase. The soapstone carving of a polar bear was now safely wrapped and in her purse.

"That's okay. Now that you're here, we can leave." The driver closed the door after her.

It was only then that Faith realized there was only one seat left open on the bus . . . and that was the seat next to Cal.

Glory, darn her, was sitting in Faith's old place beside a frowning Rhoda.

Frowning herself, Faith gingerly sat next to Cal as the bus pulled out of the parking lot.

A few minutes later, Cal dryly told her, "You lean any farther away from me and you'll end up in the aisle."

"The name of the lake we're passing is spelled T-u-t-s-h-i and pronounced *too-shy*...." the driver announced.

Too shy, that's how Faith felt. Shy and tongue-tied and restless. And sad at what she'd lost—that easy camaraderie with Cal.

It was foolish not to talk to him, she knew that. But they were past making small talk and Faith certainly didn't feel she could discuss anything personal with him. She didn't want to talk about their shared past, about their shared kiss, about the fun they'd had over the years. She didn't want to get caught up in the sticky web again.

Instead, she concentrated on her camera and the pictures she was taking. When Cal offered to switch seats with her so that she could have the window seat, she accepted with alacrity. She wasn't getting any good shots this way, the window frame was in her way.

But as Faith stood in the aisle in preparation to switch seats, the bus driver interrupted his spiel to disapprovingly say, "No standing while the bus is moving."

Since Cal had already slid into her seat, she had to try to hurriedly inch past him to get to the place by the window. Naturally, the way her luck was running, the bus turned a curve in the road at that precise instant. She almost ended up in Cal's lap, her hand grabbing hold of his thigh to prevent herself from falling.

Feeling him tense beneath her fingertips, Faith yanked her hand back as if she'd just touched a hot plate.

"Sorry," she mumbled, scrambling into her seat with more haste than grace. Her face was burning. Not because she'd touched him, but because of his reaction. He'd never tensed up like that before and she could only think of one reason that he'd do so now. He didn't want her touching him. At all. No way, no how. Things had gotten that bad between them.

Faith hid behind her camera, feigning a fascination with the pictures she was taking when the truth was that she was dying a little inside. The return trip was endless. She couldn't wait to get away from Cal. Once she'd reboarded the ship, she only stayed in her cabin long enough to dump her camera bag before heading out again. She wasn't ready to face Cal yet. She needed time to recover, to put the pieces back together again.

So she headed upstairs to her favorite location on the upper deck. She pulled open the door leading outside and was preparing to step over the raised threshold. The next thing she knew, she was falling. . . .

Seven

"**W**as accident!" Ivan exclaimed as he burst into the cabin he shared with Natasha.

"What was accident? In English, Ivan," Natasha reminded him as he lapsed into their mother tongue. "In English."

"We are in deep do-do."

At Ivan's words, Natasha's mouth dropped open.

"You said to read dictionary. I read phrase book instead," Ivan explained. "Is slang. Phrase means—"

"I know what phrase means," Natasha interrupted him. "What happened?"

"I was on upper deck—"

"Following woman, yes?"

"Yes."

"And?"

"And I think maybe she is dead now."

"Dead now? How can that be?"

"Was accident," Ivan repeated.

"What did you do?" Natasha demanded.

Ivan blinked back tears. "Was accident."

"You shot her? Stabbed her? What?"

Ivan sniffed and made no reply.

"Ivan, you said no violence," Natasha reminded him.

"Is no violence. I slipped and beeped into her."

"Beeped?" Natasha repeated with a frown.

"Beeped…bummed…bumped." Clearly agitated, Ivan waved his hands frantically. "Was accident."

"You killed woman by bumping into her? What kind of weakling is this American?"

"Do not know for certain that I killed her…." Ivan confessed.

"You stay here. I will find out," Natasha stated. "But first, what about purse? Did you get woman's purse?"

"No!" Ivan wailed.

"But, Ivan, that was entire purpose of your mission. Was not large mission. Just get purse to see if diamonds are inside."

"I thought Faith was dead…."

"Then she would not need purse," Natasha observed.

Ivan glared at her. "Am not killing machine! I have heart. I have emotions. And am not only one who has not accomplished mission here. You could not even knock out man last night in order for cabin to be searched. So do not talk of missions to me!"

"I was secretary," Natasha retorted. "Am not used to secret missions. Am not one with experience. You are one with experience." She pointed a red-tipped finger at him.

Ivan glared at her. "Do not have experience with murder. Was not in job description before."

"Do not need to murder to get diamonds back. Only need to be smart. We must work on that, Ivan. And we must study manual again. Is obvious we are not doing something correctly. Even I know that. We must get smart. Quickly."

"Why is that lady lying on the floor?" Faith heard one of the few kids on the ship ask. Her knees hurt and her hands stung. Actually, she felt as if she'd just been run over by a truck. A big one. Looking up, she saw what looked like a cast of thousands gathered around her, all staring down at her with naked curiosity. God, she hated making a scene or being at the center of one.

"Faith? My stars, what happened to you, dear?" Glory demanded as she suddenly appeared at Faith's side. To the crowd, Glory said, "Stand back and give her some air, would you? What do you think this is? A circus? Go stare at someone else."

Faith closed her eyes, wishing a trapdoor would open so she could just disappear.

"Feeling faint, dear?" Glory asked. "Somebody call a doctor!" she bellowed to the crowd.

"No!" Faith's eyes flew open and she somewhat gingerly stood up, with Glory's help. "I'm fine. I just slipped, or something...." Actually, Faith could have sworn she was pushed, but then she wasn't always the most graceful person and it was entirely possible, likely even, that she'd tripped. Other than bruising her knees and skinning her hand, she wasn't seriously hurt, although she was embarrassed as all get-out.

"Slipped?" Glory repeated with a frown. "Haven't you rediscovered your sea legs yet?"

Actually, Faith's legs were feeling decidedly rubbery at the moment.

"You're still looking a little green around the gills, dear," the older woman noted. "Perhaps I should find Calvin—"

"No!" Faith didn't want Cal hearing about this. "I'm fine."

"You don't look fine," Glory stated. "You could have broken something. Your neck, even."

"I'm sure I haven't broken anything," Faith said. "I'm fine," she assured the crowd, which was slow to depart. But then, there wasn't much action on the ship that evening, and they were apparently loath to leave the excitement of an accident site. Spotting Natasha on the edge of the crowd didn't make Faith feel any better. The other woman looked drop-dead gorgeous as always. A sleek size eight like Natasha would never trip. She glided. Compared to her, Faith felt like a clumsy elephant with two left feet.

"You could have gotten a concussion," Glory was saying. "Or knocked your front teeth out. Broken your nose or your jaw and required plastic surgery..."

"Please, Glory," Faith pleaded, wearily closing her eyes. "No more."

"You could have bitten your tongue clear through with a fall like that," Glory carried on.

"I know someone who should bite their tongue," Rhoda told Glory as she joined them. "You."

Glory glared at her. "I don't know what's come over you lately, Rhoda."

Rhoda moved to stand on Faith's other side. "I'm just telling the truth," Rhoda said.

"You don't have to do it so nastily," Glory retorted.

"I'm not nasty," Rhoda denied.

"I say you are," Glory returned.

Like bickering bookends, the two older women stood on either side of Faith, quarreling back and forth. Faith didn't think things could get worse. Then she heard Cal say, "What's going on here?"

Faith's wish for a trapdoor intensified.

"Excuse me, ladies, but I don't think you really need me here for your argument," Faith said, hoping to get away before...

"What's going on here?" Cal demanded again.

"Nothing," Faith hurriedly said, trying to forestall Glory's reply. It made no difference.

"Oh, Calvin, I'm so glad you're here. Faith has had an accident. She almost broke her neck."

"But I didn't," Faith quickly added.

As Rhoda and Glory turned to Cal to tell him what had happened, they loosened their supporting grip on Faith's arms and as a result, she began to sway a bit.

Seeing that, Cal quickly stepped forward and gently took her into his arms.

It said something about how badly she felt that Faith actually leaned forward to rest her head on his broad chest. In that instant, she felt deliciously protected.

"What happened?" Cal demanded.

Glory said, "She tripped—"

"Or something—" Rhoda inserted.

"And ended up flat on her face," Glory completed.

"*Almost* flat on her face," Rhoda corrected. "Actually, I think she fell on her knees."

Cal smoothed his hand over Faith's hair. "What about your head? Did you hit your head?" he asked her.

She shook her head, knowing she should move away but unable to deny herself this last luxury. Enfolded in his embrace...shielded from harm...treated with care. She never wanted to move. Maybe if she stood very still, this moment would last forever.

Mistaking her immobility as a sign of embarrassment, Cal tried to make her feel better by teasing her. "Sounds like you put on quite a floor show here, kid. Want to tell me about it?"

Faith stiffened in his arms before pushing him away. "Nothing to tell," she said curtly. "I'm fine."

"Sure you are," Cal retorted, not at all happy with the paleness of her face. "Come on, I'll carry you to the doctor's office."

"No way!" All she needed was Cal picking her up and cracking jokes about how heavy she was. She felt badly enough as it was.

"Okay, then I'll carry you to the cabin," he said.

"You're not carrying me anywhere," Faith stated. "I'm perfectly capable of walking on my own." She lifted her chin, daring him to contradict her.

He did, anyway. "Right," he scoffed. "I seem to recall your saying the same thing when you stepped on that nail in college. Well, I've got news for you, kid. We are not hopping to our cabin, Faith."

"We won't have to—"

"That's right," he interrupted her. "Because you're going to let me help you." Wrapping one arm around her shoulder, Cal used his other hand to support her. Although his touch was gentle, his voice was anything but as he growled, "I won't pick you up, but you *are* going to lean on me while I help you back to the cabin. Like it or not. So just shut up and get moving. One more peep and I *will* pick you up," he warned her.

The look on his face made her take his threat seriously. She went with him without any further argument. But she wasn't happy about it. Not one bit.

"Stop crying, Ivan. You did not kill woman," Natasha said as she rejoined Ivan in their cabin.

"I did not?" Ivan sniffed.

"No."

"She is in hospital, then?"

"No. She was not hurt."

"Is miracle!" Ivan looked ready to drop to his knees in prayer.

"Is *miracle* we ever got diamonds off Nabassi Island," Natasha muttered. "We have not had good luck since then. You said curse on diamonds was not true. Now I am not so sure."

"We made it to America, no? Curse did not stop us. We have come this far, can not turn back now. I told you, curse is foolish. Curse did not bother man we stole diamonds from," Ivan reminded her.

"He was overthrown. After thirty years as dictator. And *after* he got the diamonds," Natasha said.

"Was bad example." Ivan tried again. "Curse does not bother Faith. She has Midnight Ice diamonds now, but did not die when I beeped . . . bumped her."

"She does not know of curse, perhaps," Natasha stated.

"Is no matter. Curse or no, diamonds are necessary for us to start new life. Diamonds are our pension plan. We must get back."

"Did you read manual again? Must give suggestions, yes?"

"I do not know about manual, but phrase book said something."

"What? What did it say?" Natasha asked.

"Back to drawing board."

"You're making a scene," Faith muttered when Cal refused to remove his arm from her shoulders as they rode the elevator down to Three Deck.

"I'm not the one making a scene, you are," he replied. "Why is it so hard for you to accept help from someone?"

It wasn't help from *someone,* it was help from *him.* Specifically help that meant she was held smack up against him—like butter on bread. Being so close to him was taking its toll on Faith. To her way of thinking, this was cruel and unusual punishment, the equivalent of putting a drink in front of a recovering alcoholic. Too much of a temptation to someone who already had a weakness....

"You're too stubborn. Always have been," Cal was saying.

That stiffened Faith's backbone. "This coming from the man who has carried being stubborn to a fine art?"

"Takes one to know one," he retorted, helping her off the elevator. "Come on, let's get you back to the cabin so we can clean you off."

He was treating her like a three-year-old. He didn't have any idea of the kind of torment she was going through, having his arm wrapped around her waist this way. He was leaving invisible fingerprints that she was afraid would never disappear. She'd be marked for life—marked as wanting what she couldn't have.

With every step Faith took, her misery increased. She'd been doing so well. She'd held her own ground all day. Now she was losing it, fast.

They entered their cabin.

"Here we are," he said. "Now you sit on the bed while—"

"I'm not a child, Cal," Faith snapped, her endurance nearly at an end. "I'm not hurt. And I don't need any help cleaning up."

To which he simply said, "Take off your jeans."

She looked at him as if he were crazy. "I beg your pardon."

"Glory said you fell on your knees. We need to look at your knees and see what you did to them."

"*We* don't need to do any such thing."

"This is no time for modesty."

It was time for something, Faith decided. She desperately needed to get rid of him before she gave in to temptation and threw herself into his arms. "Just leave me alone," she shouted. "Go away and leave me alone!"

Cal glared at her. "Hey, if that's the way you're gonna be, fine. I'm outta here."

"You look like you could use a friend," Bud Keck told Cal as Cal sat at a table in the ship's lounge, nursing a beer. "Mind if I join you?"

"I'm not real good company at the moment," Cal warned him.

Nodding his understanding, Bud sat down, anyway. "Glory told me about Faith's accident. How is she?"

"Impossible," Cal muttered.

"Was she hurt?"

"How should I know?" Seeing Bud's startled expression, Cal added, "Sorry. Didn't mean to snap your head off. Faith claims she's fine, but would she let me check her out? No way. She got all huffy. Practically bit my head off when all I was doing was trying to help her. I didn't expect such an unpredictable reaction from Faith."

"Why not from Faith?" Bud asked.

"Because we're friends."

"She *is* still a woman, Cal."

"Yeah, I've noticed."

"You don't sound too pleased about it."

"I'm not."

"Oh, it's like that is it," Bud noted with a grin.

Cal glared at him. "Like what?"

"Nothing. Nothing." Bud hurriedly grabbed a handful of beer nuts from the bowl on the table before continuing. "You're right. Women can be impossible. I say you can't be friends with them."

"Sure you can. But it's not easy."

"I'm sure," Bud commiserated. "And being cooped up in a small cabin with one. Sheesh. When it's the woman you love, it's different. Even then...getting through all the rigamarole they put on—makeup, curling irons, eyelash curlers. My fruitcup uses an eyelash curler. You ever seen one? They look like torture devices." Bud shuddered. "I can't watch when she uses it."

"I know what you mean," Cal said, although he didn't really. He had no idea if Faith even owned an eyelash curler let alone used one. He only knew that her lashes were thick and dark, even in the morning when she just woke up and had that cute myopic look she got when she couldn't see anything more than six inches from her nose.

And now she was wearing contacts. He wasn't sure he liked her abandoning her glasses. They were a shield, protecting her from other men's interest. He sure as hell hadn't liked the looks the ship's officer had given her at the cocktail party the other evening. They were hungry, man-on-the-prowl looks. Cal knew because he'd caught himself looking at Faith the same way during the past two days.

"Tell me something, Bud. When you and Nora met, how did you know she was the one for you?"

"She made me smile. And, aside from Betty Grable pinups, she had the best legs I'd ever seen. She was at a USO dance and when we jitterbugged together...I just knew."

"Not many marriages last fifty years," Cal noted.

"That's because people expect things to be easy. Who ever claimed marriage was easy? It's not. It takes work. A lot of it. On both sides. You ever been married, Cal?"

"Me? No way."

"You're not the marrying kind, huh?"

"You got that right." His parents' messy and very acrimonious divorce had taught Cal well. No way he would put himself through that kind of hell voluntarily.

"You and Faith have known each other a long time, right?" Bud asked.

Cal nodded. "Since we were in college ten years ago."

"I haven't known her very long, but she seems like a very special young woman."

"Yeah, Faith is one of a kind."

"You know, maybe she bit your head off because she felt foolish for tripping that way," Bud suggested. "She doesn't seem the kind who'd welcome that kind of attention. Why, I remember the time we were in London, watching this fancy-schmancy parade. My wife insisted on standing on this rickety fence to get a better view. The fence fell over. She wasn't hurt, thank the Lord. But when I rushed over to help her, she just about snapped my head off. She didn't mean to, she just felt foolish. Chances are your Faith feels the same way. Go on back downstairs to your cabin and I'll bet she's waiting to apologize to you," Bud said.

"You think so?"

"I'm sure of it. What have you got to lose?"

The hot shower, now fixed after a repairman had worked on it, made Faith's physical aches feel better. But emotionally, she was still one big ache. What a mess. Here she'd come on this cruise to get her thoughts together regarding her future with Nigel and she'd ended up in a worse state than she'd been in before. And all because of Cal.

Muttering under her breath, Faith tugged on her peach-colored satin robe before carefully inserting her contact lenses. She had to blink once or twice to clear her vision. There, now she'd be able to more accurately assess the damage. Aside from looking miserable, nothing seemed amiss.

She tried putting on a happy face, but her reflection in the mirror showed her it looked more like a grimace. Muttering again, she looked down at her red, scraped hands. The left one was worse than the right. Same with her knees. The left one ached more than the right and would no doubt soon turn a lovely shade of purple. Still, all things considered, she was lucky.

She didn't feel lucky, though, as she sat on the bed and dried her hair. Emotionally, she felt as if she'd been through a meat grinder. Or perhaps a cement mixer. And she was fighting a seemingly losing battle, not only against taming her wayward hair but also against the imminent tears that threatened to dislodge her contacts.

Seconds later, the tears came and her contact lens went, which only made her cry harder.

Cal was actually whistling as he made his way down the hall toward their cabin. Bud was probably right. Faith was probably waiting for him right now, ready to apologize for biting his head off. She'd give him one of her sweet smiles and...

She was crying! Cal stood in the open doorway a moment and stared at her aghast. Faith never cried. Even when she'd had that nail sticking out of her foot.

The door slammed shut behind him as he hurried to her side. "What's the matter? Why are you crying? Is it your knee? Should I get a doctor?"

Horrified at getting caught bawling like a baby, Faith turned her back on him and shook her head. Grabbing a tissue, she hurriedly scrubbed her tears away before leaning over to quickly reinsert the one contact lens that had earlier gotten dislodged by her crying jag.

"Come on, Faith," Cal coaxed. "Talk to me."

She shook her head again. She didn't want to talk to him. She wanted to disappear.

"You can, you know. Talk to me, I mean. Just tell me what's the matter." When she still didn't reply, Cal placed his hands on her shoulders in an attempt to gently turn her around and pull her into his arms. Her reaction stunned him as she fiercely resisted his touch, shrugging it and him off.

It was the last straw. Gritting his teeth, Cal abruptly stood up. This had gone on long enough. He couldn't take anymore. Without saying a word, he grabbed his backpack from the closet and started throwing his stuff into it.

"What are you doing?" Faith demanded, finally turning around.

"So, you've found your tongue again, have you?" he said with a glare that would sizzle metal. "What does it look like I'm doing? I'm leaving."

Faith was almost afraid to ask, but she had to know. "Are you going to stay with Natasha?"

"No," he said through clenched teeth, angrily tossing another shirt into his backpack. "I'm going to pay whatever the hell it costs to upgrade to another cabin so I won't ruin your vacation any more than I already have."

Faith was surprised by his actions, but she was even more surprised by the emotion she saw on his face. Beneath the anger, there was pain and an expression of utter despair that she recognized, having seen it reflected in her own eyes as she'd stood before the bathroom mirror only minutes before.

Could it be . . . was it possible that Cal had feelings for her? Feelings more intense, more passionate than those of mere friendship?

"Why are you leaving?" Faith asked.

"Because if I stay, I'm going to end up making love with you," he told her bluntly.

"Would that be so bad?" she countered quietly, just a little surprised at her change of heart.

"It would be too good," Cal retorted. "You need someone better than me. Someone who'll marry you. You know how I feel about that."

"I know." The question was how did he feel about *her?* And she was beginning to see the answer exposed in the tormented roughness of his voice and the fierce heartache of his gaze. He wanted her.

"You need someone better than me," he repeated.

As he turned to leave, Faith stood and held her hand out to him. "I need *you,* Cal," she said. "Stay."

Eight

Cal turned so slowly that Faith felt as if she'd lived and died a thousand times before he was finally facing her. She saw the need in his eyes. Saw the passion. It was a look she'd waited years to see.

"Stay," she repeated in a whisper this time, awed by what she saw written on his face.

Her breath caught as Cal took her outstretched hand and slid his fingers between hers until their hands were entwined. She winced as he came into contact with the abrasion on her palm.

"What is it?" he asked, turning her hand over to look for himself. Seeing the injury that he hadn't noticed before, he stunned her by lifting her hand to his lips to softly kiss her wound.

That Cal should do something so loving and tender was the culmination of all her dreams. Her fingers cradled his face as she blinked away the tears.

"Does it hurt?" he murmured with concern.

Her smile broke through the tears. "If it does, only you know how to cure the pain."

Slowly, Cal slid his fingers along her arm to her shoulder, which he gently cupped as he drew her into his embrace. Feelings were expressed, although not spoken. Their visual communication was eloquent and rich with passion. He questioned. She confirmed. Releasing his hold on her hand, Cal slid both arms around her waist and lowered his lips to hers.

Now their kiss became their means of connection, enriched by the fact that Cal kept his eyes open while kissing her. Faith did the same, watching him through heavy-lidded eyes. He was so close that he was out of focus and hazy, a blur of sight and sensation.

She felt the intensity of his fiery gaze mirrored in the emotion etched on his face. Hunger. Desire. She not only saw it, she also tasted it in the thrusting seduction of his tongue, and heard it in the ragged tenor of his breathing.

When Cal tightened his hold on her, Faith did likewise, as if fearing he were a fantasy that would slip away. The silent yearning of the long years gone by were woven into her response. She kissed his ear, his jaw, his left cheekbone, his temple.

Likewise, his mouth rushed over her face, chasing after pleasure points, pressing urgent kisses against every throbbing pulse. He wrapped his hand in the silken curtain of her hair, twining his fingers through the wild curls and lifting them out of his way as he nibbled his way toward the nape of her neck.

She undid his denim shirt, smoothing her hands up over the muscular warmth of his bare chest. She was shaking inside with wonder at this newfound freedom to explore. He was everything she wanted and more. Her desire for him was laced with a love and a sense of possession that frightened her. Until she stared into his blue eyes and saw the same mix of emotions there. Desire . . . possession . . . these things intensified in his heated gaze as he unfastened her robe. When he looked at her, Faith felt more beautiful than she ever had in her entire life. Such was the power of his look, as real as a touch.

Having unwrapped her as if she were a priceless treasure, Cal proceeded to cherish her. He cupped the creamy swells of her breasts, holding her in the palm of his hands, while brushing his thumb over her nipples, caressing first one rosy tip...then the other...then both simultaneously. Faith felt the anticipation building as his mouth hovered over her willing flesh.

She closed her eyes, breathless with excitement as he gathered one aroused peak into his mouth, bathing it with the velvety roughness of his tongue. Sliding her fingers through his hair, she curled them tightly with each successive wave of exhilaration incited by the erotic lap of his tongue.

The next thing Faith knew, they were both lying on the bed. She had no clear recollection of how she had gotten there or how Cal had gotten rid of his remaining clothing, not that she cared. She was where she'd always longed to be. In his arms. In his bed. With nothing between them. She felt as if she'd finally met her destiny.

Cal couldn't believe she was really in his arms. After all they'd been through, he thought he'd never have her there again. And the very real possibility that he'd lost her had been festering inside him, eating away at him.

Why hadn't he seen her sooner? What had taken him so long, he wondered, awed by the way she fit beneath him, by the lushness of her curves and the rightness of their embrace. She came so vibrantly alive when he kissed her, responding with an open and giving passion that Cal found irresistible. His old-time buddy was gone and in her place was an incredible woman, a new Faith.

Any lingering doubts Cal may have had were heading right out the porthole window. Because this need was too overwhelming for him to fight any longer. Did he even want to? Or was it more that he wasn't sure how she felt? He needed to clear something up before they went any further.

"I'm not Nigel," he reminded her with a growl.

"I know," Faith whispered. "You're Cal. Impossible, stubborn, and the man I . . ." She stopped.

"Yes?" Cal prompted her.

"The man I want."

Words were abandoned after that in favor of kisses that spoke of hungry need and caresses that expressed fiery desire. Faith was awed by the discovery that she could shatter his composure the same way he'd shattered hers earlier. Brushing her lips over his heartbeat made it race out of control. Tasting him with her tongue made him shiver. Nipping him with her teeth made him growl. Exploring him with eager hands made him grow even more taut with need.

Feeling incredibly daring and tipsy with her newfound power, Faith lifted her arms to his shoulders, relishing the feel of his bare skin against hers, her breasts brushing his chest with every breath she took. And she was breathing *very* fast, excited by the intense pleasure of his touch.

Murmuring her name, Cal lowered his mouth to hers, capturing her provocative smile and measuring the sultry sweetness of the roof of her mouth with the tip of his tongue. Using his hands, he reexplored the smooth outward curve of her breast, taking his time and adoring every creamy millimeter as he made his way toward the rosy crest. Once there, he discovered the sweet little sighs of pleasure she made as he again rubbed his thumb over the puckered tip. When he leaned down to tease her with his tongue, her sigh became a breathless moan. Threading her fingers through his hair, she held him to her.

Surveying her with his lips, Cal sent his hands on a scouting mission of their own, seeking out her feminine secrets. She tightened her hold on him as he caressed her with first one finger . . . and then two . . . in an intimate seduction whose rhythm was as old as time. She was damp and hot, smooth, like silk.

Cal couldn't wait any longer. Protection. The thought entered his mind long enough for him to make a grab for his jeans and his wallet. Moments later, he was back with her.

He kissed her once again, his tongue mimicking the melding movement soon to come. His hands returned to wreak havoc on her senses, delicately rubbing against the nub hidden in the crisp bed of curls between her thighs, propelling her from one plateau of pleasure to another. Faith was out of control. Wanting him...needing him within her, she reached for him and guided him safely home.

He came to her in a sliding rush, one continuous motion of ecstasy. She tightened around him, welcoming him until he was lodged deep inside her. The rhythmic clenching of her inner muscles almost drove him over the edge.

Cal opened his eyes, concentrating on the flushed passion in her face, the dazed joy in her eyes. It gave him the strength to hold on a little longer, to make sure she'd truly reached her climax before he gave in to his own. Only when he felt the tremors take hold deep within her, growing until they filled the universe, only then did he surrender to his own release, shouting his pleasure.

"Was that my stomach growling or yours?" Cal lazily inquired several hours later.

Resting her head against his bare chest, Faith turned to look up at him. "That's what happens when you skip dinner. The midnight buffet should be going on about now," she said with a glance at the bedside clock.

"Then we'd have to get dressed and that would be a crime."

"Going to the midnight buffet *without* getting dressed would be a crime," Faith retorted with a saucy grin.

"I don't want to share this view with anyone," Cal stated, running his hand over her bare shoulder.

"So what do you suggest we do? Starve?"

"No. I've still got a surprise or two up my sleeve yet," Cal murmured.

"You're not wearing any sleeves," she observed.

"You noticed."

"Mmm," she murmured, leaning across his chest to kiss his left arm. His right arm was firmly wrapped around her.

"You know, I don't think we'll be hearing any more ice hitting the ship like we did that first morning," Cal stated with a wicked smile.

"Why not?"

"Because we generated enough heat to melt several glaciers, let alone icebergs."

Faith tried not to blush. By his teasing laugh, she knew she hadn't succeeded. Feeling suddenly self-conscious, she said, "In the morning we dock in Juneau. I booked a tour of the Mendenhall Glacier. You can get very close... it's supposed to be magnificent."

"*These* are magnificent," Cal murmured, lowering the sheet to caress her bare breasts. "And I'm enjoying getting very, very close." He trailed his fingers across her skin, skimming the soft surface with teasing intent. "They are certainly worthy of a very detailed tour...." But before he got very far, the sound of their stomachs growling in harmony made both Cal and Faith crack up.

"Sounds like we better get some food into you before you faint dead away from hunger," Cal said with a rueful grin.

"I certainly don't want that happening," she stated, reaching for her robe, which was pooled on the floor. "Collapsing once in one day is plenty."

"Did you feel faint then? Is that what happened?" Cal asked her.

"No. You know," she mused aloud, "I could have sworn that I didn't trip, that I was pushed."

"Pushed?" Cal's grin faded entirely, replaced by a look of grim concern.

"I probably just imagined it," she reassured him before admitting, "I'm not exactly the most coordinated person."

"I don't know," Cal murmured, his smile slowly returning. "You looked pretty coordinated when you raced onto the bus this afternoon after hitting me with that snowball."

She looked at him with an expression of confused innocence. "What snowball?"

"The one you threw at me on the White Pass."

"I didn't throw it at you," Faith denied.

"Come on. I saw you give me that triumphant grin."

"Because I saw the snowball hit you and thought you deserved it. That didn't mean *I* was the one who threw it. You know, there was that teenager sitting in the back of the bus with his parents. The sullen one. I'll bet he was the one who threw it at you."

Cal eyed her skeptically, but her look was so guileless that he eventually believed her.

Faith saw the moment when he was convinced. Only then did she say, "Gotcha!" Her triumphant grin mirrored the one she'd given him on the White Pass. "And you said I couldn't bluff," she scoffed before sailing off into the bathroom.

Despite having known her for ten years, Cal was rapidly discovering that Faith was full of surprises. What would the next one be?

Half an hour later, they were sitting in bed, Cal wearing the bottom half of his navy pajamas, Faith wearing the top half, which reached midthigh. On a tray between them was a pizza topped with salami and artichoke hearts that Cal had special-ordered from room service.

"I can't believe you did this," Faith said in between bites. "I haven't had one of these in ages."

Looking at her, sitting there so adorably, with her glasses perched on her nose, Cal was reminded of those earlier days, ages ago, when as college students they'd shared pizzas and dreams. She was the first to know about his dream of being a journalist and the only one to hear his real reasons, his desire to put a spotlight on the world's inequities. At the time, he'd laughed self-consciously; a cynic like him wasn't supposed to have such quixotic goals, let alone entertain such lofty idealism in the eighties, a time when monetary gain was supposed to be one's number one consideration in life.

Faith hadn't laughed. She'd just looked at him and smiled. And she'd believed. In him.

"You're incredible," Cal murmured huskily.

Confused by his words, Faith looked down at the now-empty pizza pan. "Sorry. I ate more than my fair share, didn't I?"

"No, you didn't and that's not what I meant."

"What did you mean, then?"

"That you look incredible," he replied, reaching out to run a finger down the open V-neckline of his pajama top she was wearing. "I'm glad you're wearing your glasses again."

"You are?" This surprised her. "What on earth for?"

"Because other guys don't make passes at girls who wear glasses. Besides, I always liked the way you scrunch up your nose when your glasses start sliding down. Makes you look like a little rabbit."

"You're too kind," she retorted mockingly. "It's always been my aim in life to be told I look like a rabbit."

"A sexy rabbit."

"Oh, that's lots better," she said, rolling her eyes in exasperation.

"I can see I'm going to have to convince you."

"You can try," she replied.

"Ah, you know I can't resist a challenge." Setting the tray on the floor, Cal reached over to slide his hand around the nape of her neck and draw her closer. "Let me try this again. I'll rephrase my last compliment. You look great," he said huskily, continuing to caress her nape with his fingertips while holding her captive in his hungry gaze.

Faith could feel her cheeks growing warm, not to mention other portions of her anatomy.

The too-large pajama top slid off her one shoulder, drawing his attention and his kisses. He nibbled his way from her neck to her shoulder tip and back again, scraping her skin with the edge of his teeth. Faith shivered, never expecting to feel such excitement from what had seemed at first to be such a simple caress. But nothing with Cal was simple. For the first time, she realized that complexity had its advantages.

With his eye for detail, Cal took note of her reaction, the way she tilted her head allowing him further access, the way her lips curved into a sexy smile. He took his time exploring and expanding his study to new territory, adding the curve of her jaw and the sensitive hollow beneath her ear.

Swirling his tongue around the shell of her ear, he whispered enticing promises in between erotic little licks. When he took her glasses off, she breathlessly reminded him, "I'm blind as a bat. I can't see."

"You don't have to see," he huskily assured her, placing her hands on his body. "Just feel your way around . . ."

She did, with deeply satisfying results for them both.

Faith and Cal were late getting up on deck the next morning. To save time, they ate outside at the buffet breakfast offered in the café. Cal stood in line to get their food while Faith searched for an empty table. Finally finding one, she sat down and saved it for herself and Cal.

She was so busy waving her location to Cal, who was still at in the banquet line, that she didn't realize Ivan had joined her until he spoke.

"I heard you had accident yesterday," Ivan said, standing nervously beside her table. "You are not injured, I hope?"

Faith shrugged. "I'm okay. My knee is black and blue and I bruised my hand a bit." She held up her palm, which she'd bandaged that morning.

Ivan turned pale. "Am sorry. Very, very, very sorry!" he exclaimed with heartfelt contrition.

Faith frowned. "You mean you're sorry about that incident in your cabin?"

"That, as well, yes. I mean, yes, of course . . . yes, I was referring to incident in cabin. What else?" He shrugged nervously and rubbed at his mustache as if hoping to erase it. "Nothing else. No, of course not. Nothing else. I humbly offer my apologies. Was wrong of me to act so. Please forgive me for such behavior. It pains me much to have you think badly of me."

Taking pity on his obvious agitation, Faith asked, "How is your back today?"

"Is nothing compared to the heaviness in my heart. Tell me you forgive me. Is important to me."

"We'll forget it ever happened," Faith agreed. "But that doesn't mean I plan on making any more visits to your cabin, if that's what you're thinking."

"I am thinking nothing," Ivan assured her. "Nothing at all. Am thinking nothing."

"That I can believe," Cal muttered as he joined them with a tray in his hands. But before he could say anything further, Ivan scurried off.

"You scared him," Faith said.

Cal showed no remorse. "Good. I meant to. You never did tell me what happened between you two that night you had dinner with him."

"And you never told me what happened between you and Natasha," Faith retorted.

"Nothing happened."

"You're sure?"

"Positive. What about Ivan?"

"We had a . . . misunderstanding, that's all. We cleared it up just now."

"You better not be planning on spending any more time with him," Cal stated with a warning frown.

"And you better not be planning on spending any more time with Natasha," she returned.

"Why would I want to when I have you?"

"My point exactly," Faith said with a jaunty grin. When Cal looked at her that way, she felt confident enough for ten women!

"Oh, so you two are talking to each other again," Glory noted, having just caught Cal and Faith sitting together, cuddling in the back of the tour bus that was going to take them around Juneau and then out to the glacier.

"You could say that," Faith replied with a smile.

"Something is up," Glory declared. "But I'm not going to ask you about it. Because, despite what Rhoda says, I am not a busybody."

When Faith and Cal didn't say anything, Glory glared at them.

"Of course you're not a busybody. You're just a people person," Faith belatedly replied.

"But we're still not going to tell you anything," Cal inserted. He gave an *oomph* as Faith gave him an elbow in his side.

"What Cal meant to say was that we're glad you're valuing our privacy," Faith clarified.

"Yeah, right," Cal murmured.

"Take your seats, please," the guide said over the intercom. "The sooner everyone gets seated, the sooner we can get on our way."

"And the sooner we get on our way, the sooner we can get this tour over with and go back to our cabin for the important stuff," Cal whispered in Faith's ear.

"Juneau is the state capital, despite the fact that in 1974 the people of this state voted to move it to a more accessible location, closer to the big cities of Anchorage and Fairbanks," the guide stated. "The city is accessible only by air or water as the Juneau Ice Fields block any access by road."

"Access," Cal murmured, surreptitiously sliding his hand beneath her pink mohair cardigan to sneak in some very sexy caresses. "Now there's a fascinating subject."

Faith lost track of the guide's commentary after that. She vaguely heard the guide end by saying something about there only being four stoplights in town when she suddenly exclaimed, "You've got to be kidding!" as Cal's seductive brand of teasing almost took her breath away. They were sitting in a busful of people here!

"Four stoplights is more than we have in my home-town," Glory said turning around to tell Faith.

Faith nodded and tried to smile at Glory, while grasping Cal's hand firmly in her own to prevent any further explorations on his part.

"Party pooper," Cal said.

"You think so?" She shifted their clasped hands to his lap, where she did a little exploring of her own until Cal was the one to call it quits.

"I hope you learned your lesson," she said.

"You'll have to keep teaching me so I won't forget," he returned with a grin.

"Juneau is located in a hollow where it rains more than it snows," the guide began again as the bus headed out of the city. "And it rains here two days out of three. The mountains behind the city mark the beginning of the Juneau Ice Fields and are a barrier, providing a natural shelter against the bitter cold. So the climate here is actually milder than the rest of Alaska, although milder is a relative term.

"The town is built long and narrow to fend off the winds," their guide continued. "Along the winding streets that lead up the mountainside from the central city area, there are handrails to hold on to when the gale blows in off the Taku Glacier."

As the bus traveled the thirteen miles toward the Mendenhall Glacier, Faith couldn't help but remember the last time she'd been on a bus tour—was it only yesterday? The idea was mind-boggling. So much had changed in such a short period of time. She and Cal were lovers now. When she'd been in Skagway, she'd still relished hopes of getting over him. Now she had hopes of a future together.

Not that they'd talked about the future. It was as if they'd both made an unspoken pact to focus on the present and not worry about the future. It was a pact Faith had no intention of breaking, especially when the here and now was so incredible.

Feeling his eyes on her, Faith turned to find Cal staring at her with a new kind of intensity. "What are you looking at?"

"You. I'm looking at you."

"Is something wrong?" For a moment, Faith wondered if she'd somehow gotten a smudge or something on her face.

"Nothing is wrong." With his free hand, Cal traced the curve of her cheek, taking great pleasure in seeing the delicate shade of pink tint her creamy skin. Why hadn't he ever noticed the incredible beauty of her blush before?

The lyrics to a popular song came back to him, something about the thing you're looking for being the one thing you can't see. Faith had been right in front of him all these years, yet he hadn't really seen her until now. Hadn't appreciated her special beauty.

Cal would be the first to admit that he still wasn't altogether comfortable with the suddenness of his attraction to Faith or his inability to control his feelings. He'd never liked being at the mercy of his needs, physical or otherwise. He still wasn't sure what this emotion was that he felt for Faith...and he wasn't too eager to analyze it yet. It was special and that was enough for now.

Cal knew himself well enough to realize that if he thought this was love, he'd be liable to panic and screw things up. And he didn't want to do that. So he put a lid on the uncertainty, preferring to bask in the warmth of Faith's smile.

"Am brilliant!" Natasha exclaimed as she rejoined Ivan in their cabin.

"You found diamonds?"

"No, but will soon. Told woman ship is departing at four in afternoon."

"Woman?" Ivan repeated in confusion.

"Faith. We have been discussing any other woman?" Natasha demanded in exasperation. "No."

"You told Faith ship is departing at four? That is brilliant?"

"Is brilliant when ship departs at two in afternoon," Natasha returned with a smug look. "Cal and woman will be left on dock as we leave. Left behind in Juneau."

"No one will be in their cabin," Ivan continued, finally catching on.

"And we can search cabin in peace."

"We have had too much stress, that is problem," Ivan said. "We need time to do good work. Is not good to be rushed."

"This way, we will have time to search cabin way it should be searched. Like professionals. No rushing."

"Am not doing well with rushing," Ivan agreed. "Incident of yesterday is leaving me shooken."

"Shaken," Natasha corrected him.

"Do not correct me. I know how I feel. Is shooken. Was sure I had killed her. We must proceed cautiously now. Cannot make any more mistakes. Stress is not good for me."

"It's a lovely view, isn't it?" Glory said as she joined Faith and Cal in the Chapel-by-the-Lake, the first stop on the tour.

Faith nodded her agreement before taking yet another photograph. The log chapel was built near the edge of Lake Auk and had the best view in all the world. Or at least the best Faith had ever seen. The picture window behind the altar framed the incredible sight of the magnificent Mendenhall Glacier in the distance. The mile-and-a-half-wide glacier was reflected with mirrored perfection in Mendenhall Lake in the foreground. It was a photographer's dream.

"Maybe you and Faith will come back and tie the knot here," Bud said with a sly smile in Cal's direction.

Faith's heart sank at the distant expression that appeared on Cal's face at the mere mention of tying the knot.

Apparently Nora saw it, too, for she quickly reprimanded her husband.

"Now, honeybear, you leave those two alone," she said, the red apple earrings she wore dangling back and forth as she shook her head at him.

"Ah, fruitcup, I was just teasing them," Bud defended himself.

"It isn't polite to butt in to other people's business," Glory loftily informed him.

Which made everyone crack up.

"What's so funny?" Glory demanded.

"Nothing," Nora hurriedly assured her. "Come along, honeybear. We'd better get back to the bus."

Although Faith was smiling along with everyone else, that momentary look on Cal's face at Bud's mention of marriage remained in her mind's eye—niggling at her peace of mind.

"Did you see the look on Glory's face when the guide told her to use the outhouse while we were at the glacier," Cal asked as they strolled down the street in Juneau. After returning from the bus tour, they'd decided to find a nice place in which to have lunch.

"It wasn't the fact that it was an outhouse. What upset her was the fact that the door had been ripped off by bears," Faith said. "To quote Glory, 'I've heard of air-conditioned facilities but this is ridiculous!'"

"I'm telling you, the look on her face was priceless," Cal stated with a grin.

And so it may have been, but it was the look on Cal's face that continued to stay with Faith—the look he'd gotten at the chapel when Bud had mentioned marriage. Try as Faith did, she couldn't seem to get it out of her thoughts. It had distracted her while they'd visited the area around the glacier, which had loomed in the background—looking closer than it was. Their guide had said that this was a common occurrence, that distances were hard to gauge when dealing with glaciers.

Other things were also hard to gauge, like Cal's thoughts. Except for his views on marriage, which were crystal clear. As to how he felt about her... no words had been spoken. He hadn't said he loved her, but then she hadn't said she loved him, either. And she did love him. Tremendously.

"How about here?" Cal asked.

"What?" Faith looked around in surprise. They'd come to a halt in front of a seafood restaurant along the waterfront.

"How about eating lunch here?" Cal said.

"Sounds fine."

After they'd been seated at a table near the window and had placed their orders of fried clams and coleslaw, Cal said, "You seemed a million miles away a few minutes ago."

"Sorry about that. I was just thinking..."

"About what?"

"About dreams. Did you notice the men hanging around the bars we passed?"

"No, and you're not supposed to be noticing other men, either," he said with a disapproving glare.

"I wasn't noticing them that way. I was referring to the looks on their faces. Those three men weaving down the street looked the same way. It was the look of someone whose dreams have been shattered."

"Their dreams probably have been shattered. A lot of people came up here during the booming oil years, hoping to make a fast buck. Some did make it rich, and some blew their money. Some never even made it that far."

"It's sad." Faith had found it particularly sad in light of the fact that her own dreams regarding Cal had come true. She was sitting here with him across the table from her, smiling at her in that special way she found so incredible.

They had just gotten their order of fried clams when Faith noticed the Kecks hurrying past the open doorway of the dining room, apparently having just come from the section of the restaurant that offered fresh Alaskan crab shipped to your home. Nora spied Faith and pulled Bud to a halt.

"What are you two doing?" Bud asked from the hallway.

"Eating lunch," Cal replied.

"You better get a move on," Bud said.

"Why? What's the rush?"

"We have to be aboard the ship in five minutes."

Cal turned to Faith. "You told me it didn't leave until four."

"That's what Natasha told me," Faith replied, distinctly recalling Natasha's providing that information when Cal had left to get information on the location of their tour bus.

"Well, she must have gotten it wrong with the language problem and all," Bud said. "The ship leaves at two. And trust me, they leave on time and they don't put the gangplank back down for anyone. A friend of ours got stranded in port after she was only ten minutes late. She didn't have anything with her but her purse and they just took off, anyway. She stood there on the dock crying, and that captain didn't do diddly-squat except to yell down at her that she shouldn't have been late. We gotta go. You two better hurry or you'll miss the ship."

A second later, the Kecks were gone.

Cal immediately signaled their waitress but there wasn't time to do more than slap a twenty on the table and slide their fried clams into a plastic freezer bag Faith kept stored in her purse whenever traveling.

"Keep the change," Cal told the startled waitress as he and Faith went running out of the establishment.

"Brilliant plan did not work!" Ivan announced, having returned to their cabin from his position along the railing on the upper deck. "They just boarded ship."

Natasha muttered several colorful phrases in their mother tongue. In English, she exclaimed, "Is curse. Is Midnight Ice curse!"

"What are you saying?"

"Am saying that we are cursed. No matter what plan we make, it does not work. There is no other explanation."

Ivan was getting uncomfortable now. "Do not say such things. You will bring bad luck."

Natasha snorted. "You believe in bad luck, yet you do not believe in curse? Is not logical, Ivan."

"Is not my job to be logical."

"Is your job to find diamonds."

"Nerves are shocked...shot...am nervous. Look at hands...." Ivan held them out to her to show her the tremor shaking his fingers. "Cannot hold binoculars to do surveillance. Cannot use secret tool to unlock cabins. Cannot sleep at night."

"Cannot sleep because room is too stuffy," Natasha inserted. "Would be better if we had windows. Is like closet in here."

"Yes, is like closet, but is not reason for my upset. Is because of guilt. Am feeling guilty to have hurt Faith."

"You did not hurt her," Natasha denied.

"She has hand in bandage."

"Could have arm in sling," Natasha said. "That would be hurting."

"You are cold woman," Ivan accused.

"Is not true! I do not like situation any better than you do," Natasha retorted. "Am not trained for such things. Reading manual is not same as doing things."

"This we found out when you could not even do simple thing like slip the man a mickey in drink."

Natasha glared at him. "Is useless for us to argue."

"Am beginning to worry is *useless,* period," Ivan stated morosely.

For once, Natasha did not contradict him.

Nine

———

"**I** can't believe how close we came to missing the ship," Faith said as she and Cal stood near the railing on the upper deck. "They took up the gangplank right after we boarded."

"It was close," Cal agreed. Holding out the plastic bag containing their hastily gathered lunch, he said, "Want a fried clam?"

Between them, they finished off the clams in no time at all. Cleanup was provided by Faith, who found a few packets of wet wipes in the bottom of her purse. "What else do you have in there?" Cal asked in amusement. "First the plastic bag, now these...."

"I wish I had a slingshot in here. If I did, I'd use it on Natasha."

"A little upset, are we?" Cal inquired.

"It's not funny, Cal. We could have missed the ship."

"But we didn't. So stop worrying about it. If you want to worry about something, worry about our ship clearing that one over there." Cal pointed. "Because from here, it doesn't look like we're gonna make it."

Faith immediately leaned over the railing to get a better look.

"Hey, be careful," Cal said, grabbing her arm and pulling her back.

"I was going to take a picture," she protested.

"You were going to end up in the drink. Just stay back here where I can keep an eye on you."

"I'm not a child—"

Cal stopped her protest by kissing her. It was brief, but it made his position clear. He was treating her not as a child, but as the woman he cared about. "You've already taken one fall," he reminded her huskily. "I'm not willing to risk any more accidents happening to you. So humor me, okay?"

"Okay," she agreed with a tremulous smile.

"Yoo-hoo, Calvin! I'm so glad I found you," Glory breathlessly exclaimed as she joined them. "Actually, I'm glad I found Faith. She's the one I need to speak to for a moment. You don't mind, do you, Calvin?" Glory had grabbed hold of Faith's arm and dragged her away to a private corner of the deck before Cal could say a word.

Faith braced herself for one of Glory's inquisitions, but to her surprise Glory wanted to talk about Ivan.

"You see, I'm considering asking him to the Western Night party this evening," Glory explained. "You know, where everyone gets dressed up in Western attire and we do square dances and things like that. You and Cal are going, right? You have to. So, anyway, about Ivan—what do you think he'd say? Do you think he'd accept my invitation?"

Before Faith could form a reply, Glory barreled right on. "I mean, you don't think that would be too forward? Because heaven knows I don't want to be thought of as pushy. Not that I'm shy, either. I admit that. But I'm not pushy, either."

Faith struggled to come up with the right thing to say.

Glory clearly took Faith's silence as approval because she said, "You're right, of course. I *should* ask him. Thank you, my dear—" Glory patted Faith's hand "—thank you for helping me make up my mind."

"I didn't do anything," Faith said.

"Certainly you did. You listened. That's rare in young people these days. What are they babbling about down there?" Glory frowned down at the officer on the bridge directly below them. "I can hardly hear myself think. Those walkie-talkie things are so annoying. Oh, my stars, did you hear that? They said we're not going to clear—"

"I heard it," Faith said, listening to the voice over the walkie-talkie saying, "Okay, maybe we'll clear…yeah, it's okay."

"My stars, they don't drive any better than I do," Glory exclaimed. "I'll bet that young navigator isn't pleased about you and Cal. I just hope he keeps his mind on his job. Well now, enough chatter. I've got to go find Ivan." With a wave, she was off.

Faith stayed where she was for a few more moments, taking several action shots as their ship turned 180 degrees, just missing the bow of the cruise ship waiting to take their berth while another cruise ship remained at the dock. As if that wasn't enough, Faith counted seven floatplanes—looking like mosquitoes sitting out there in the water—either landing or taking off from the harbor.

"Busy place, isn't it?" Cal noted as he joined her, trailing his fingers down her cheek. "What did Glory want? Don't tell me she tried to give you the third degree again."

"No. She was asking me about Ivan."

"What about him?"

"She wondered if she should invite him to the Western party tonight."

"What did you say?"

"I didn't have to say anything. In the end, Glory made up her own mind."

"Why does that not surprise me?" Cal murmured.

"She thinks we're going to the party, as well."

"Actually, I was considering it," Cal admitted. "I planned on getting you a feather boa and a lace garter...."

"Really? I thought I'd wear jeans and go as a cowgirl."

Cal looked so disappointed that Faith had to laugh. The truth was, she had a blouse and skirt that could be transformed into a saloon girl outfit without much trouble. Besides, now that she knew Cal was as affected by her as she was by him, she wasn't about to pass up this opportunity to make the most of the situation and tempt the living daylights out of him.

"What's so funny?" Cal demanded.

"You'll see later," she promised him. "You'll see...."

"Yoo-hoo, Ivan!" Glory called out with an energetic wave.

"Oh no," Ivan muttered to Natasha. "Is dragon woman."

"Be polite. Do not act suspicious. Be calm," Natasha advised him before slipping away.

"She deserts me, like rat on sinking ship," Ivan grumbled to himself. "Ah, lovely lady—" Ivan's voice immediately changed as he greeted Glory "—how good to see you again." For an additional flourish, he leaned over to kiss her hand.

"I've been looking for you, Ivan," Glory said with a flutter of her false eyelashes. "I wanted to ask you something...."

"Was not me," Ivan immediately declared, backing off. "Whatever happened, was not me."

Glory patted his hand solicitously. "There now, you're in America now. You don't have to be so nervous anymore. I was just going to ask you if you'd join me at the Western Night party this evening. I was nervous myself about asking you but then I spoke to Faith—"

"She is attending party?" Ivan interrupted Glory to ask.

"She and Cal are, yes, I believe so." Glory eyed him suspiciously. "You're not still harboring any ideas about Faith, are you, Ivan?"

"Ideas?" Ivan repeated.

"She and Cal have made up and are clearly in love. They may have been friends before, but they are definitely more than that right now. Why I never saw a cuter pair of lovebirds."

"Lovebirds? You are bird-watcher? You are talking about something you saw through binoculars? Like bald eagles?"

"Never mind," Glory said. "You haven't answered my question. Will you come with me to the party tonight?"

"Yes, I will be there."

"Good. All you have to do is dress up in a pair of jeans and a checkered shirt and you'll fit right in."

"Good. That is good. Am looking forward to fitting in," Ivan said. "Goodbye for now, lovely lady."

"What did woman with pink hair want?" Natasha asked as she rejoined Ivan a short while later.

"She invited me to Western party tonight. She also said that Cal and Faith are lovers now. So plan you had to seduce Cal will no longer work."

"I could get his attention in minute...."

"We will finish discussion later," Ivan stated with a warning look at their crowded surroundings. "Must not be overheard. Do not need more troubles."

"Oh, look, Cal! You can see the glacier now." They'd been cruising down Tracy Arm Fjord for the past hour and the ship had just rounded a curve in the sheer-walled valley, leading to an incredible view at its end.

To Cal, one glacier pretty much looked the same as the next, but Faith clearly didn't feel that way. It was the photographer in her, no doubt, Cal noted with some amusement—watching as Faith headed straight for the railing with the other shutterbugs. She'd taken his advice to heart, however, not leaning over the railing but keeping a respectable distance.

The wind had picked up and it was getting nippy, making Cal glad he was wearing his thickest sweatshirt. Of the several hundred passengers on board, only forty or so diehards were willing to face the elements in order to see this view, which he had to admit *was* pretty incredible now that he looked at it. The late-afternoon sun was just hitting the massive white glacier, flooding it with light while the shadowy sides of the mountains bracketing the ice field provided a dark frame.

The ship's cruise director came on over the loudspeaker system. "Alaska has more than half of the world's glaciers. However, in ten years of cruising, this is the closest we've ever been able to get to this particular glacier. You people are indeed very fortunate."

Cal felt fortunate, fortunate to be sharing this experience with Faith. Those expressive eyes of hers were glowing with excitement as she beckoned him over for the group shot the ship's photographer was quickly setting up to record this milestone. Cal wrapped his arm around Faith, smiling at the way she snuggled into him even as she was fussing at him for not being dressed warmly enough. It was vintage Faith.

After most of the others had drifted away, Faith remained to take a few more photographs of the snow-capped mountains in the ever-changing light. She was so excited that Cal had to admit he got a kick out of just watching her. And every so often, she'd toss this smile over her shoulder at him, a smile that shared everything she was feeling and warmed his heart, as well as other regions farther south.

Once she'd put her camera away in the camera bag at her feet, Cal came to stand behind her. Tugging her back against his chest, he wrapped his arms around her—one over her shoulder, one placed snugly around her waist.

Faith leaned her head back to rest it on his shoulder. His arms provided a band of security, love and protection. This was heaven: being in his arms, warmed by his body, feeling cherished. This wasn't lust, and it wasn't just attraction. This was the real thing. Something timeless . . . and as majestic as the surrounding scenery.

She sought out his hands with her own, matching their location as she placed her left hand atop his left hand where it rested just below the swell of her breast, his fingers curving around her rib cage. She then slid her hand down his right arm, the one that was draped over her shoulder and chest, until she reached his hand, where she intertwined her fingers with his.

She never wanted to move, unless it was to snuggle back more closely against him. Like the mountains sheltering Juneau, Cal was sheltering her. Faith smiled at the analogy. She'd never considered herself to be a fanciful person before, but right now she was feeling downright poetic.

Who knows how long they would have stayed that way had a sudden shout from behind them not drawn their attention. "Oh, no!" wailed Bud Keck as papers came flying out of his camera case. The gusty winds immediately scattered the papers to the four corners of the earth. "My traveler's checks!"

Faith made a grab for one that flew by her, but to no avail.

Cal immediately yanked her back from her somewhat precarious position leaning over the railing. "They're only traveler's checks. They're replaceable. You're not," Cal reminded her.

"Good thing I only had twenty dollars in cash in there," Bud noted.

Around the corner, Ivan grabbed the twenty dollar bill that flew past him. "Look! Is good luck! Is sign from above!"

"Is from rodent-killing man," Natasha retorted, pointing toward Bud. "Honeybear is his name."

"Money is ours now. We need more than honeybear does. If we do not find diamonds by time we reach Vancouver, we will need to watch pennies. Could be we will be on street with no money. Homeless. Living in boxes, like peoples we saw on TV from satellite dish on Nabassi."

"Do not panic yet, Ivan," Natasha said.

"When is time to panic, if not now?"

"I will tell you when is time to panic. Until then, keep calm. Look, Cal and woman are over there. This would be good time to check cabin..." Natasha paused to swear in her own language. "They are leaving now. Is too late. We are always too late."

"Keep calm," Ivan reminded her. "We will return to cabin now and make plans. We have lucky twenty dollar now. Luck is going to change for us."

It hadn't taken much for Faith to turn her off-the-shoulder organdy blouse and red taffeta skirt into attire suitable for a saloon girl. Her black hose not only hid her black-and-blue knee, but also went well with the red lace garter she wore. Her legs were amply displayed as she bunched up her calf-length skirt on one side, using her marcasite half-moon pin to hold it in place just above her knee. The delicate cameo that hung from a black velvet band around her neck was the perfect finishing touch. A pair of matching antique cameo earrings dangled from her ears.

She'd used a slightly heavier hand with her eye makeup, a dark mauve powder that made her seem more exotic and mysterious. She'd pinned her hair in place with several strategically placed barrettes. A light misting of her rose-water perfume and she was ready.

Opening the bathroom door, she stood with one hand propped on her hip as she flashed Cal her best flirtatious look. To her utter delight, his jaw actually dropped open. Gaining confidence, she sidled up to him, tiptoeing her fingertips along his arm. "Hey, cowboy, wanna dance?"

"You look... incredible."

"You don't look so bad yourself," she noted, admiring the way he filled out a pair of jeans and a denim shirt, his favorite everyday attire. His only concession to the dress

code of the festivities was the red bandanna he'd tied
around his neck.

"I think this is going to be a very memorable night," Cal
murmured. "Very memorable indeed."

"You are sure I fit in?" Ivan demanded as he stood beside Natasha, tugging on the silk paisley scarf he wore
around his neck. His jeans were brand-new and stiff as a
board. He'd deliberately worn his best silk white socks and
his black evening shoes, highly polished just that afternoon. He'd asked the clerk at one of the ship's stores for a
"checked" shirt. The red-and-white one he wore reminded
him of the tablecloths outside on the upper deck.

"No one is looking at you," Natasha informed him,
preening by swishing her long hair over her shoulder.
"Peoples are looking at *me*."

Faith was one of the people looking at Natasha, who was
also wearing an off-the-shoulder style top. In fact, her entire outfit was more *off* than on. Made entirely of gold lamé
and formfitting in the extreme, Faith wondered how the
other woman could even breath in it, let alone sit down.
The skirt was a micromini. A place mat would use more
material.

The dancing had already started by the time Faith and
Cal had arrived. Without so much as a glance in Natasha's
direction, Cal swept Faith up and led her right into the
Texas two-step on the dance floor.

It was the first time Faith had ever danced with Cal.
While they'd attended some of the same social functions in
college and even afterward, they'd never danced together.
It was her own fault; in her freshman year, Faith had refused Cal's first invitation to dance with him, and he'd
never asked her again. She'd been nervous of making a fool
of herself, of stepping on his feet, of giving her feelings
away.

Now there was no time or need to be nervous as he
smoothly led her through the simple steps.

"I've got a surprise for you later," he whispered in her ear.

"You do?"

Cal nodded. "I thought we'd leave early and stop by the casino..."

A tap on his shoulder made Cal turn around. Looking down a few inches, he saw Ivan standing there. Ivan said, "I believe is custom to tap shoulder and exchange partners for dance, yes?"

"No," Cal returned.

"That was rude," Faith noted as Cal swirled her away.

"You wanted to dance with him?" he retorted.

"No. Absolutely not."

"You never did tell me where the two of you disappeared to that night we all met for drinks," Cal said.

"It's not an evening I care to remember," Faith replied.

"Parts of it were incredibly memorable," Cal returned, kissing her ear. "Having you in my arms, kissing you... I did know it was you, by the way. The only reason I said Natasha's name is that she was the one who'd brought me back to the cabin. I could never get the two of you confused."

"That's for sure," Faith noted with a quick look in Natasha's direction. "I'm two of her."

"If you mean you're twice the woman she is, then that is certainly true," Cal replied.

"Twice the woman she is in what way?"

"In every way that counts." The look Cal gave Faith said it all.

"Ivan, we haven't danced yet," Glory told him.

"Am sorry. Do not feel well. Must return to cabin," Ivan stated.

"But... Drat! He got away again," Glory muttered. "My stars, that man is more slippery than a greased pig."

Down in their cabin, Ivan and Natasha were planning their next course of action.

"Cal and Faith are going to casino after dance," Ivan said. "I heard him say this to her. Now is perfect opportunity to search cabin."

"Why must *I* be one to search cabin?" Natasha demanded. "*You* have more experience. You should be one to do that job. I can stand in casino and be lookout. This is perfect dress for job." She smoothed a hand over her gold lamé outfit.

"You just want to look at Cal," Ivan accused her. "You want to make puppy-dog eyes at him."

"I do not make puppy-dog eyes," Natasha returned, straightening to her full height and glaring at Ivan.

"Yes, you do. I have seen you do this." Ivan made a goofy face, almost crossing his eyes in the process.

Natasha was infuriated. "If I wanted Cal, I could have him like that." She tried to snap her fingers but her long nails got in the way.

"I told you. He and Faith are lovers now. Your attempts to get information from him about missing diamonds was failure."

"Your attempts to charm woman was also failure," Natasha reminded him.

"Only because of war injury to back."

"You were never in war!" Natasha snapped. "You strained back while moving furniture in party headquarters fifteen years ago. You forget, I read your files."

"And I read yours. So do not give me trouble. I will be lookout and you will search cabin."

"I will be lookout and you will search cabin," Natasha repeated his words, changing their meaning when *she* said them.

"That is right."

"Good." Natasha headed toward the door. "I will come down to warn you if they leave casino. Good luck with searching cabin." Before Ivan could say a word, she was gone.

Ten

___

"I can't believe you haven't come to the casino before," Cal said as he led Faith inside.

"I looked in the door once," she admitted.

"That doesn't count."

"I feel badly for leaving the dance early."

"We're not the only ones who did," Cal noted.

Following his gaze, Faith saw Bud and Nora Keck, as well as Glory. "Hey, howz it going, you two?" Bud asked them. "That Western band drive you outta there, too? I love country and western as much as the next man, but it's gotta be in tune. You know what I mean? Those guys weren't even coming close!"

"I prefer big band music," Glory said. "You can dance to that. Not that my partner stayed around long enough to dance with, anyway," she added with an angry sniff. "I don't know why I let you talk me into inviting Ivan, Faith. It was a big mistake."

"Me? But I didn't—"

"The man has no manners. I'm not going to waste my time on him. I gave him his chance and he blew it. He's not going to disappear on me again. And he's not the only one. Rhoda has been going off on her own lately, as well. If I were the suspicious kind . . . but I'm not, so I'm not going to dwell on it. Besides, I just got some good news."

"You did?" Faith said.

"They announced it at the dance. You must have missed it."

"Cal and I did step outside for a few minutes . . ." Faith trailed off, remembering what they'd stepped outside for—a little privacy and a few fiery kisses.

"Well, they announced the winner of that contest I told you about, the one about Alaska. And it was me," Glory stated proudly. "I won. Forty-nine dollars since Alaska is the forty-ninth state."

"Congratulations, Glory," Faith said.

"Thank you." Glory beamed. "I came here to double my winnings."

"But what if you lose?" Faith asked with a worried frown. "Gambling is a risk."

"Listen, at my age, life is a risk," Glory retorted before leaving to head toward the cashier's cage in search of some change.

"You ever been in a casino before?" Bud asked Faith.

"No. Does it show?"

"A little," Bud said. "My little fruitcup and I go to Atlantic City a couple times a year to play the slot machines. Right, fruitcup?"

"That's right." Nora shook the disposable cupful of quarters that she held in one hand. "And I always wear my good-luck grapes." She wiggled her head and set her sterling silver dangling grape earrings moving. "So we're all ready. Good luck, you two. Come on, honeybear."

As the Kecks headed toward one of the brightly lit slot machines, Faith turned to Cal. "I'm not a very good gambler," she admitted.

"How do you know?" he countered. "You've never done it before."

"I'm not the luckiest of people."

"I have this feeling your luck is about to change. Besides, you've always been competitive. I remember those Ping-Pong matches we used to have in college. You were deadly."

Faith grinned. "I admit, I like to win. But I can't control the winning with a slot machine."

"Come on, try it. You'll like it."

"That's what you said when you had me try that Indian curry dish you concocted for that dorm party our sophomore year."

"And it was delicious."

"I couldn't tell," she retorted dryly. "My taste buds were numb for a month afterward."

"Nothing ventured, nothing gained."

He was right, as usual. After all, she'd taken a chance with him and look how well it had turned out. Nothing ventured, nothing gained. "Okay." She took the quarter he held out to her. "I'll give it a try, but I'm really not very good at this..."

When he let himself into Cal and Faith's cabin, Ivan was still muttering under his breath, wondering how Natasha had twisted things around so that he'd ended up being the one to get this job.

"Is not fair. I am one in charge," he muttered as he closed the door behind him. "I should be one giving orders. Natasha needs to be learning who is in charge here. She thinks she can fool me. She cannot. Is all her fault valuables are missing in first place." Ivan opened the closet and looked inside. "What is this?" He lifted a small case from one of the built-in shelves. "Is locked. I have found valuables! Must be in here." Ivan turned to leave, then paused. "Is better I make sure valuables are inside," he decided. "As Natasha says, we have not been having good luck." Using his tools, Ivan began working on the lock.

Half an hour later, he finally got the case open. "Is...computer. Not valuables." Ivan sighed in disappointment before giving the computer another look. "Is very, very small computer. Have never seen one this small. Have seen pictures, of course." Fancying himself something of a technical expert, Ivan turned the notebook computer on, murmuring, "Perhaps there is clue about valuables on computer. I wonder...how much memory does hard drive have...."

"What do you mean we're out of quarters?" Faith demanded, her cheeks flushed with excitement. "I just won thirty dollars ten minutes ago."

"And you lost it all again," Cal returned. "It's time to quit."

"Not yet. I'm going to win next time. I know it! I can feel it!"

"Here." Glory loaned her a quarter. "Just be quiet, would you? You're distracting me."

"Thanks, Glory. I'll pay you back."

"What happened to the clear-thinking woman who guards her money like a hawk?" Cal demanded.

"You took her into a casino and gave her a taste of the fast life," Faith retorted, sliding Glory's quarter into the dazzling slot machine.

"I'd rather have a taste of you," he murmured, nibbling on the sensitive skin right beneath her left ear. He slid his arms around her the way he had on deck earlier—one arm around her shoulder, the other around her waist. "I think you need some fresh air to clear your mind."

"What you're doing is clouding my mind, not clearing it," she told him.

"Are you complaining?"

"I lost!"

"Oh, I wouldn't say that...."

"Cal! What are you doing?" she demanded as he took her by the hand and practically dragged her out. "I only need one more quarter..." Faith exclaimed with a longing look over her shoulder at the rows of slot machines.

Cal stopped so abruptly, she smacked into him. Cupping her face with his hands, he kissed her, tempting her as only he could. "Which would you rather play with?" he inquired with a wicked grin. "A slot machine or me?"

"No contest. Let's go!"

"So, you are *very* rich man?" Natasha was asking a heavy roller who'd just won big-time at the blackjack table. She looked up just as Cal and Faith were hurrying out the casino's door.

Swearing in her own language, Natasha dumped the heavy roller she'd picked up and raced over to follow Cal and Faith. She saw them get into the elevator, heard Cal saying something about their cabin right before the elevator doors closed. She quickly looked around but couldn't find a house phone to call Ivan and warn him.

Kicking off her four-inch high heels, Natasha had no choice but to dash down the three flights of stairs leading to Three Deck. She knew the elevators were almost as slow as the ones on Nabassi.

Ivan was coming out of their cabin just as she raced down the hallway. She could hear the ping of the elevator arriving. "Hurry. They are coming now." Grabbing Ivan by the arm, she rushed him around the corner, where they stood just out of sight at the end of the hallway as Cal and Faith kissed in front of their cabin before going inside.

"Disgusting," Natasha muttered. Turning to face Ivan, she said, "Did you find valuables?"

"No diamonds. He has nice computer, though. Has 120 meg of memory...."

"You searched entire cabin and found no diamonds?"

"Could not search entire cabin. They came back too soon."

"You were coming out of cabin when I arrived."

"Because back was getting bad. Need hot water bottle on it. Could not bend down, so could only check area above here..." He made a motion with his hands at about his waist-level.

"Is curse," Natasha raved. "We *are* cursed!"

Faith and Cal barely made it back to their cabin before their passion got the better of them. The second the door closed, Cal backed her against it and started kissing her. Faith welcomed his embrace, immediately sliding her hands up his chest to clutch his shoulders and hang on as she became dizzy with desire.

Murmuring her name, Cal scattered the pins from her hair, threading his fingers through the curls as his mouth fused with hers once more. Faith tightened her hold on his shoulders, her fingers clenching a handful of his denim shirt. The hunger was as intense as ever. He inspired it in her and she in him. That much was clear from the passionate way their mouths came together in a kiss that was blatantly sensual.

Cal tilted his head first one way, then the other; experimenting with angles, discovering newfound pleasures in the taste of her tongue; priming her for their ultimate joining and making her blood boil using nothing more than his kisses.

Her fingers dug into his skin as the ache within her intensified. She nipped his bottom lip with her teeth, seducing him as he was seducing her. The next thing she knew, Cal had lifted her in his arms, and her legs were around his waist.

Now their embrace was fueled by the feel of him, taut and throbbing at the apex of her thighs. Her skirt was bunched up, and the rub of his denim jeans against her silky panties was enough to drive Faith into another realm of reality—where nothing mattered but having him within her.

Cal felt as if he were going to burst. Driven beyond reason or control, he reeled toward the bed where they landed in a tangle of arms and legs. Faith found herself propped on top of him and made the most of her position by unfastening his jeans, sliding them and his jockey shorts out of the way enough that his arousal could spring free. Cal helped her by lifting his hips even as he was reaching for her bit-of-nothing silky underwear, ripping it from her body at her request.

They reached for the box of condoms together, tearing it open and raining packets all over the bed. His hands shook as he slid on a condom. So did hers as she helped him.

And then he was there, sliding deep within her, lodged near to her soul. The pleasure was so intense it was almost painful, causing Faith to cry out his name.

Fearing he was hurting her, Cal paused, but she urged him onward with her words and her hands. Bracing her hands on his shoulders, she smiled down at him. Grasping her hips, Cal surged upward in a thrust that propelled them both from this world to another.

For Faith, the surge of motion shattered the tightening anticipation into a thousand pulses of raw pleasure.

For Cal, her climax triggered his own.

It seemed like aeons later before either had the energy or coherence to form complete sentences—and even then, they were brief.

"You okay?" Cal murmured, brushing the hair from her eyes as she lay collapsed on his chest.

"Mmm. Can't believe . . ."

"Me, neither."

"We're still dressed." Her whisper held equal parts of mortification and satisfaction.

"Sorta."

"May never move again," she mumbled.

"I wouldn't bet on that."

"Betting and gambling is what got me into this situation in the first place." It was the longest sentence she'd formed so far and she celebrated that fact by kissing the underside of his jaw.

"Let's try that again," Cal murmured. "Only slower this time. And without our clothes."

Faith showed her approval of his plan by unbuttoning her blouse and tossing it over her shoulder. He helped her with her bra, although the truth was he was more of a distraction than any real help. His shirt was next, and she repaid him in kind, taunting him with her fingertips, raking her nails over his bare skin each time she undid one of his buttons. The remaining three buttons went flying as Cal tore his shirt off.

"Slowly," she reminded him with a sultry smile as his jeans soon joined his shirt and her clothing on the floor.

"Slowly," he agreed with an outlaw's grin.

She was awed by the fact that he remembered things that pleasured her, like brushing his thumbs over the tips of her breasts and caressing her in a certain way.

"The first time was fast and furious," Cal whispered in her ear, swirling his tongue around the lobe and making her shiver with delight. "This time..." He reached down to tempt her with his fingers, delicately stroking the rosy folds, dewy with desire. Tempting her more and more...only leaving her in order to don protection. "This time..." He came to her in a slow progression that drove her to distraction, joining his flesh with hers. "This time I thought we'd explore..." He groaned as she moved against him. "Explore...some of the...finer points of cruising—" he moved deep within her "—the Inside Passage."

"Explore?" she whispered breathlessly. "Like this?" She matched his rocking motion.

"Oh, Faith!"

Neither one of them could speak after that, their gasps and moans expressing their increasing passion. Faith closed her eyes, her senses saturated in a rapture that went beyond mere sensations. The erotic friction of his sliding thrusts, the rolling motion of the ship, the vibration of the ship's engines—everything merged into one incredible moment. Faith felt it coming, closer, closer, building...each convulsive ripple of ecstasy building on the last until the waves washed over her and through her, drowning her. She surrendered gladly and with a smile of infinite satisfaction on her lips.

For Faith, that last day on the cruise ship went by in a blur. She and Cal opted to explore each other rather than the town of Ketchikan, although they did go ashore long enough for Faith to pick up a T-shirt that said, Alaska, Home of the Individual and Other Endangered Species. Cal got one, too.

That evening, Bud ordered a bottle of champagne to be delivered to the table at dinner. "It's been a great cruise. I can't believe it's almost over already," Nora noted with a shake of her head. She was wearing her red cherry jewelry set again. "Can you, honeybear?"

"Me, neither, fruitcup."

"I can't believe Rhoda jumped ship in Ketchikan with our twenty-two-year-old wine waiter," Glory said with a shake of her head. "She was always such a stable sort."

"Still waters run deep," Cal reminded her.

"You can say that again," Glory muttered.

"Well, let's drink a toast," Bud suggested, lifting his glass. "To everyone's good health and happiness."

"Am dying, I tell you. Dying!" Ivan moaned.

Natasha matched him moan for moan. "Was fish we ate in town today. I told you was no good."

"You told me nothing."

"Out of my way," Natasha demanded as she stumbled into the bathroom.

"Where is medicine doctor gave us for food poisoning?" Ivan said, bamming on the closed bathroom door. "Do you need to be so loud when you are emptying stomach? Hurry up, you are making me ill again. Is my turn to use bathroom now. Natasha, hurry!" Ivan put his hands over his ears...and then over his mouth...before grabbing Natasha's empty tote bag just in the nick of time. After throwing up, he zipped the bag closed. Looking up, he saw Natasha standing in the bathroom doorway. "Was emergency," he stated weakly.

"I will show you emergency..."

"I don't want this to end," Faith murmured as she and Cal stood on the upper deck, viewing the sunset. Her words were the closest she'd come to talking about their future.

But Cal failed to pick up on them and Faith wasn't willing to risk ruining the moment by getting into a heavy discussion about what would happen once they returned to Seattle. That time would come soon enough.

For now, it was all too easy to believe that they were the only ones in a magical world shimmering with color. Even though it was after eleven, the sunset was still showing off. The coastal mountains in the distance were dark silhouettes drawn against the chromatic sky, the horizon ablaze with fiery ribbons of red, one color bleeding into the next, red merging with orange to yellow to light blue and ending in indigo.

"The last frontier," Faith murmured. "It looks so vast and invulnerable."

"But it's not. Invulnerable, that is. The disastrous oil spill from the tanker *Valdez* brought that home with a vengeance. A buddy of mine covered that story. Said he'd never seen anything like it."

Faith shivered, recalling the images she'd seen on her TV screen of the affected wildlife. She'd sent a donation to Greenpeace the very next day.

"Some things need special care," Cal noted with a slow smile. "You're a good example."

"Me?"

"Yes, you." Cal gently combed his fingers through her hair. "You need special care. If we go down to our cabin, I'll show you what I mean." His soft kiss was tempting. So was her response.

They didn't speak again until they'd returned to their cabin and had completed their preparations for bed.

"It's strange to think we'll be leaving the ship for good in the morning when we dock in Vancouver," Faith murmured as Cal joined her on the narrow confines of his twin bed.

"I prefer to concentrate on doing a little preliminary docking of our own this evening," he murmured in return. "I thought we might practice a few maneuvers...." He unbuttoned the pajama top she was wearing. "Like charting our course...." He brushed his index finger from her lips to her chin, the chin that lifted whenever she was ready to do battle with him, continuing in a straight line to the underside of her jaw and down the contour of her throat to the hollow above her collarbone.

His caress was all the more potent for the fact that he was only touching her with one finger, sketching a make-believe line as he continued down the shadowy valley between her breasts. Faith shivered when his hand brushed her breasts in passing, before he continued on his tempting course over the curve of her stomach, hopscotching over her navel to the line of her silky underwear. There he stopped. She looked at him in anticipation.

"Once we've set our course," Cal said huskily, "the next step is to stoke the boilers...."

"This ship has boilers?"

He quirked an eyebrow at her. "You prefer to engage the engines?"

She pretended to consider the matter. "A difficult choice. Better demonstrate them both for me."

He did, sliding his hand beneath the lacy waistband of her panties to comb his fingers through the crisp hair hidden there. His smile had that desperado edge she loved so much as he dipped his finger into her moist warmth. One finger gradually became two, slipping in and out, creating a friction and a rhythm that made her blood sing

"I think we're ready to proceed full steam ahead...." His caresses became even more intimate, seeking and then finding the ultra sensitive little nub that would bring her pleasure. Brushing his thumb against it, he watched her shiver in his arms.

But Faith wasn't about to leave him behind. She wanted him to feel the same kind of tense excitement she was feeling.

"Full steam ahead," she murmured in sultry agreement, sliding his pajama bottoms out of her way in order to measure him with her hands, cupping him in her palm before slowly sheathing him in a condom.

"Next step is maintaining position...." Cal growled, as he remained poised, the tip of his arousal at the very brink of her inner passage, nudging her in the most incredibly sensual way possible.

"Then lowering the anchor...." With one slick surge, he came into her fully. "Before we sink... Yes. Oh, yes...we sink...together."

Surrendering to the surges of sheer ecstasy, Faith cried out his name as he shouted hers before collapsing on top of her.

Despite the wickedly teasing nature and banter of their lovemaking, Faith sensed a certain desperation in the way Cal held her afterward. Her last thought before she fell asleep was that they still hadn't talked about what would happen once the cruise was over.

The alarm didn't go off the next morning, so they woke up late and had to rush to get packed. Faith felt all thumbs as she hurriedly grabbed her clothes off the hangers in the closet and tried to fit them all back in the suitcase.

This always happened to her. She knew the clothes fit in that suitcase at the beginning of the trip, but they showed no signs of fitting now. It didn't help matters any that Cal had finished his packing in five minutes, simply stuffing his things into his backpack. Sighing, Faith impatiently pushed her glasses back into place, there hadn't been time to put in her contact lenses, and then tugged the hem of her pink sweater down over her hips. Neither action quelled the uneasiness growing within her.

Cal's silence this morning was making her nervous. It seemed that the closer they got to Vancouver, the quieter he'd gotten. Perhaps he was tired? Perhaps he had regrets? Perhaps he was aggravated with her for not being able to close her damn suitcase—she shoved the lid down and snapped it closed. Now all she had left was her tote bag. She zipped that shut with no problem.

"Do me a favor? Would you make sure I got everything from the nightstand?" Faith asked Cal. "I'm missing that brochure I got in Ketchikan yesterday."

Cal silently checked out the nightstand and the area around it before saying, "I didn't find the brochure, but I did find this." He held up his discovery. "Your face cream, I presume?"

"Where did you find it?"

"Wedged between the nightstand and the edge of the bed, near the floor."

"I wonder how on earth it got down there."

Cal just shrugged.

"Thanks." She took it from him, telling herself she was imagining the way he seemed to avoid touching her as he handed it over. Upset by the incident, she stuffed the face-cream jar in her purse.

Cal said, "I told you you'd imagined the whole thing about your face cream being stolen."

Faith wondered if she'd *imagined* the passion between them, as well. Because there was no mistaking the coolness in the air. It had been increasing the closer they got to Vancouver. She tried to start several conversations with him to no avail. Finally, she said, "Are you okay?"

"I'm fine," he said curtly. "Why?"

"Because if I didn't know better, I'd say that you were acting like someone who has regrets." When he didn't say a word, Faith's heart sank with the realization that Cal was acting as if he had regrets because he *did* have regrets. Big-time regrets.

Eleven

"**Y**ou *are* having regrets, aren't you." Faith didn't even voice it as a question. There was no need to. The answer was written all over his face. Discomfiture. Uneasiness. "I see," she whispered, her voice strangled.

For Faith, it was New Year's Eve all over again. Cal was pushing her away, only this time it was after they'd shared the most intimate experience two people could share. They'd made love. At least, *she* had. *He'd* apparently just been having sex with her.

It hurt. So much so that she was numb. Her throat tightened painfully, as if someone had fastened a clamp around it. She went cold all over. In some distant corner of her brain she realized her shivers were caused by shock. Faith couldn't believe this was happening to her. After all that she and Cal had been through.

What exactly had they been through? she asked herself bitterly. Ten years of friendship, off and on, plus a few nights of incredible sex. That's all it had been for Cal. Sex. Nothing more. A fling.

And now, he was clearly afraid that she was going to cling. Make things difficult. That's why he was distancing himself from her. Why he'd been so cool and aloof this morning.

Dummy that she was, she hadn't taken the subtle hint. No, she'd had to go and ask him outright, making matters worse. But she honestly hadn't expected him to confirm her worst nightmares. She'd actually been hoping and praying that he'd deny them. Only he hadn't.

Instead, he'd stood there, with those damn walls of his now firmly back in place. Any access he'd previously allowed her was cut off. He clearly didn't want her reading his thoughts. Aside from that brief moment when she'd seen the misgivings reflected in his eyes, he'd shielded his thoughts as surely as if he'd encased them in lead.

Gathering her tattered pride, Faith reached for her packed tote bag while haughtily informing him, "There's no need for you to have any regrets, Masters. I don't. The truth is that I've had a crush on you since our college days and I've always wondered what it would be like to make love with you." She shrugged. "Now I know, and I've gotten that curiosity out of my system. End of story. So don't worry about me, Masters. I'll be just fine. Wish I could say it's been fun, but it's certainly been educational. And it's over." An instant later, she was gone.

Cal was stunned. He couldn't believe what Faith had just said to him. She'd had a crush on him? Since college? She'd only made love with him out of curiosity?

An image flashed in his mind's eye, that evening after they'd first made love when Faith had flashed a triumphant smile at him after fibbing about not being the one to have thrown that snowball at him. "Gotcha," she'd said. "And you said I didn't know how to bluff...."

Yeah, she'd gotten him good, all right. With both barrels. So he'd had a few regrets. Hell, he was only human, after all. You couldn't turn around twenty years of thinking overnight. His distrust of marriage and long-term relationships ran deep. He'd told her that. She'd said she understood.

For twenty years he'd had it drummed into his head. His dad had approached the topic from a dozen different angles, telling him that marriage is like a bath. Once you've been in it awhile, it's not so hot.

Well, the way Cal was feeling now certainly wasn't so hot, either.

He still couldn't believe that she'd had a crush on him. He'd had no idea. Sure she'd kissed him that one New Year's Eve in college, but he'd thought she was tipsy. God knew some idiot had poured enough booze into the punch that night to make her so. He'd figured she didn't know what she was doing. He'd thought he was doing her a favor by pushing her away.

Hell, he'd felt uneasy and guilty about that episode for weeks afterward. Not that he'd let her know it. That wasn't his way. But he'd made damn sure not to give her any hint of the way he felt. Because it had been easier to pretend nothing had happened rather than to face the possibility that he cared about her other than as a friend. He hadn't known how he'd felt then. But he knew how he felt now.

Cal had to accept the very real possibility that he loved Faith and that was why he'd panicked this morning. Why he'd withdrawn from her. Hell, it wasn't a possibility. Or even a probability. It was time to quit kidding himself. He *did* love her.

When she'd accused him of having regrets, Cal hadn't known what to say, so he didn't say anything. His feelings about marriage hadn't changed, yet his feelings for Faith had. He regretted the loss of the status quo in their previous relationship and the simplicity that had entailed, but that didn't mean he regretted the fact that they'd made love. It also didn't mean he was ready for matrimony yet. But he needed to talk to her, to sort things out.

Because the bottom line was that Faith wasn't the kind of woman to make love with a man merely out of curiosity. She'd only make love with a man she loved. He'd come to grips with his feelings, it was time she came to grips with hers. Because despite what she'd said, Cal wasn't buying her claim that it was over between them. He refused to let that happen.

"I cannot believe you ruined tote bag," Natasha was complaining to Ivan as they both joined the crowd disembarking from the ship into the customs hall.

"I replaced bag," Ivan retorted. "We must keep lookout for Faith. Do not want to lose her now."

Since Natasha was several inches taller than Ivan, she was better able to look over the crowd. And what she saw made her go pale. "Ah, Ivan. Remember when I said would tell you when was time to panic?"

"Yes."

"Is time to panic now, Ivan."

"What is wrong? You are getting fearful of crowd?"

"No. I am fearful of *them.*" She slid her eyes to one side.

Ivan frowned before realizing she was signalling something to him. "Them? Where?" He stood on tiptoe. "Cannot see."

"Over there." She pointed to two hulking men standing on the other side of the glass, near the exit leading to the buses waiting to take the passengers from the customs hall to the airport.

The crowd shifted enough for Ivan to catch a brief glimpse of them. "They are from Nabassi. What are general's men doing here?"

"What do you think?" Natasha retorted impatiently. "General sent them to get stolen valuables back. From us. And we do not have valuables."

"Is only one thing we can do," Ivan said with a quick look around.

"Run?" Natasha suggested hopefully.

"No. Ask Faith for help."

Faith was impatient to get out of the customs hall, to get to her car and just drive away, putting this entire cruise behind her. She hung on to her anger the way a drowning man would hang on to a life preserver. If she allowed the despair to take over, she'd surely drown in it and be lost.

At least she'd never told Cal she loved him. She had that much to be thankful for. It was small comfort.

"Next," the customs agent called out.

Faith went through the formalities with no holdups. Finally, she had some luck on her side. She didn't want to see Cal again, which was why she'd purposefully made sure she was one of the first to get through customs. It wasn't like her to be so forceful, but one thing this cruise had done for her was to teach her to stick up for herself. No more going along to get along. No sirree. She deserved better.

Faith was heading for the luggage claim area when she was waylaid by a clearly agitated Ivan and a frantic-looking Natasha.

"Is urgent we speak with you," Ivan told Faith. "Is matter of life and death."

"What's wrong?" she asked.

"We are ones," Ivan blurted out. "Ones who stole face cream. From your room."

Faith frowned, barely following his rapidly spoken words. "You stole my face cream?"

"From bathroom, yes. We thought was our face cream."

"I don't understand."

"In beginning of cruise, you got bag, bag that was ours," he impatiently explained. "When we got bag, face cream was missing. Diamonds in face cream were also missing."

Diamonds! Faith's mouth almost dropped open as she suddenly recalled the jar of face cream Cal had found that morning, wedged between the nightstand and the bed...near the floor...where it could have rolled after she'd spilled the contents of the mysterious tote bag that first day on the ship. The tote bag that hadn't been hers ... and had apparently been Ivan and Natasha's.

"We were just looking for our valuables," Natasha inserted. "Everything we did ... was only to retrieve valuables."

Ivan nodded vigorously. "That is right. Am also one who beeped into you."

"Bumped," Natasha corrected him.

"Am sorry," Ivan rushed on, ignoring Natasha's comment. "You said you forgave," he reminded Faith. "Now is time to prove and help. Men are after us. Chasing us. We need help to escape. Men work for dictator and want to hurt us. Badly."

"What did you do to make them chase you?" Faith asked.

"Steal dictator's diamonds," Natasha said.

"Was not exactly steal," Ivan amended. "We just took. Diamonds were sitting there, country was in mess, dictator overthrown. Is no time now to explain. Will you help?"

Faith didn't know what to say. It was an incredible story.

Apparently having gotten impatient with Faith's hesitation, Natasha moved closer and the next thing Faith knew she felt something that felt suspiciously like a gun being poked in her back. Looking over her shoulder, Faith realized that Natasha had her right hand in the pocket of the trench coat she was wearing. "We have no time," Natasha exclaimed, jabbing Faith with the hard object again. "Is best you do what we ask," she said in a threatening tone.

That did it. Faith had had enough for one day. First Cal, now this! She was tired of getting pushed around. "Listen, sister," Faith growled, "I've already had a hell of a day and I'm not in the mood for this."

"Sister?" Natasha repeated, bewildered by Faith's reaction, having clearly expected her to fold in terror.

"Shut up, Natasha," Ivan instructed her curtly. "You are going to ruin everything! Put lipstick away. She has no gun," Ivan quickly assured Faith. "Show her," Ivan ordered Natasha, who reluctantly held out her empty pocket and clutched her lipstick. "I may be fool sometimes, but not foolish enough to give Natasha gun," Ivan assured Faith.

"Once I am done reading manual..." Natasha muttered.

"If we do not leave now, we will not be reading anything," Ivan retorted sharply. To Faith he gave a pitifully woeful look. "We throw ourselves on your mercy. Will you help?"

"Is your fault we are in trouble," Natasha told Faith. "You stole diamonds from us."

"Quiet, Natasha. Now is not time. Faith, you will help us, yes? Valuables are no longer important. You may keep. We will forget all about them if you will help us."

Faith saw Ivan's fearful look at a pair of bruisers standing near the buses leaving for the airport.

"She will help us," Natasha assured Ivan. "She does not want our death on her conscience."

A week ago, Faith would have hurried away and never gotten involved. But the new Faith believed what they had to say and was willing to take a risk. Something inside of her trusted that Ivan and Natasha wouldn't hurt her, despite Natasha's stupid prank with the lipstick tube. Faith wasn't foolish enough to tell them she had the face cream and therefore the diamonds in her purse, however.

"All right. I'll help," Faith declared. "With conditions."

"We agree," Ivan hastily inserted. "Whatever you want, we agree."

Natasha immediately nodded, as well.

"Fine," Faith said. "Then listen closely..."

Trying to find Faith in this crowd of what had to be a thousand people was like trying to find a needle in a haystack, Cal noted in disgust. He'd lost her. But only temporarily, he told himself. Once he talked to her and cleared some things up....

But he had to find her first. He'd searched high and low for her on the ship before realizing she must already have disembarked, along with several hundred other passengers from their ship, not to mention an equal number disembarking from another ship. He thought he'd caught sight

of her curly hair up at the head of the customs line a few
minutes ago, only to lose her again.

Frustration churned within him. He knew she had her car
parked here in Vancouver and he needed to reach her before she started driving back to Seattle.

A flash of color caught his eye. Faith had been wearing
a bright pink sweater.... Yes, it was her!

Cal impatiently moved forward, but the line through
customs was being held up by someone who had apparently tried to smuggle through a bag of fresh fruit. Now
everything and everyone was held up while the woman ar-
gued her case and inspectors searched her bags.

Cursing under his breath, Cal shouted Faith's name. She
turned around. "Wait for me," he ordered her.

"Take a long walk off a short pier, Masters," she
snapped, and took off with two strangers, a tall one in a
baseball cap and a short one wearing a babushka and a
trench coat.

"Don't tell me you two are at it again," Glory said. She
was standing behind Cal in the still-unmoving line.

"Faith and I had a slight misunderstanding, that's all,"
he maintained.

"A misunderstanding? Looked like she wanted to see
you drawn and quartered," Glory said.

The Kecks were standing in the line running parallel to
the one Cal was in. Bud leaned over to speak to Cal in a
strictly man-to-man undertone. "Remember what I told
you about relationships. It ain't easy. But it's worth it in the
end," Bud added, stepping back to hug his wife. "Don't
give up."

"I don't intend to, Bud," Cal muttered. "You can count
on that."

"Plan worked!" Ivan exclaimed as he sat scrunched up
in the small back seat of Faith's hatchback car.

"I told you it would," Faith said as she started the car.
"No one would recognize either one of you in those get-
ups." She looked at them and couldn't help but be im-

pressed with her handiwork. She'd only had the contents of her tote bag to work with, after all. And the clothes Natasha and Ivan had already been wearing.

A quick trip to the bathroom with Natasha had resulted in Natasha wearing the baggy Alaska sweatshirt Faith had bought as a gift for Chris and a pair of Faith's jeans, which the slinky Natasha had had to hold up by sticking her hands in the pockets and slouching forward. On her head, Natasha wore the baseball-type cap Faith had picked up as another gift for Chris. Her long dark hair was stuffed inside the cap, which was tugged down low over her face—a face that had been scrubbed clean of makeup and now looked pale and washed-out. Natasha's three-inch heels had been replaced with a pair of Faith's sneakers.

Ivan's costume had consisted of Natasha's discarded trench coat, which reached his ankles, a scarf wrapped around his head like a babushka and the crowning touch of Natasha's heels. Ivan had rolled up the cuffs of his slacks to his knees while he'd been in the bathroom. He'd also shaved off his mustache, a traumatic occurrence for him but no more so than the thought of being at the mercy of the two bruisers waiting for them outside. For good measure, Faith had handed him her retro sunglasses. She figured they hid a lot of Ivan's face and they might give him confidence.

It worked. He hadn't wobbled in the high heels once, although he had to practice taking baby steps.

"Ivan looks good in high heels, no?" Natasha noted with a smile.

"As good as you look disguised as boy in cap," Ivan retorted.

Natasha immediately moved to take off the cap, but Faith stopped her. "Keep your costumes on. Both of you. Until we get to my place in Seattle. We don't want to take any risks. When we cross the border from Canada to go into the States, the officials there will see you."

"But we do not match our passport photos this way," Natasha said.

"Oh. Right." Faith frowned. "Okay, then keep the disguises on until we're out of Vancouver. You can take them off when we get near the border."

"You are good at this," Ivan complimented her. "Perhaps you would like to join us...."

One quelling look over her shoulder disabused Ivan of that notion. "Was just suggestion."

"I've already got a career, thank you very much," Faith said. "A life of crime is not for me."

"Was not successful for us, either," Ivan acknowledged.

"Which is one of the things we're going to talk about when we get to my place. Until then, just sit back and relax."

By the time Cal got out of the customs hall, there was no sign of Faith. He knew in his bones that she'd already left. His next step would have to be catching up with her at home. Unfortunately, that took longer than he'd hoped, as his flight was delayed. Cal would have rented a car and driven, but there was a convention in town and rentals were hard to come by without a reservation.

In the end, he took the flight, but it was almost four in the afternoon by the time he pulled up in front of Faith's apartment building on the outskirts of Seattle. They'd left the ship at nine that morning. It had been a long day and one he didn't want repeated.

Knocking on her front door brought no response. Neither did ringing the bell. So he started pounding with his fist. "Come on, Faith. Open up! I know you're in there, your car is out front. I'm not going away until you open this door." His tactics worked. He heard the locks being undone. The door finally opened.

Only it wasn't Faith standing there. It was Ivan. A very disheveled-looking Ivan, with his shirt hanging open and looking for all the world as if he'd just gotten out of bed.

Twelve

"Where's Faith?" Cal demanded in a dangerous growl, pushing Ivan aside and storming into the apartment.

"In shower," Ivan replied.

"In the shower?" Cal repeated, unable to believe what he was hearing or seeing. Surely Faith hadn't taken up with Ivan on the rebound? Not in six hours. No way. It didn't make any sense.

But then Cal figured that nothing had been making much sense lately: his falling for Faith, her claim she'd only slept with him out of curiosity, and last but certainly not least, Ivan standing in her living room...with lipstick on his collar.

Cal's feelings were too primitive to describe. He only knew that he was damn tempted to react like one of those heroes in the medieval romances Faith favored, and skewer someone, preferably Ivan.

"Listen, you little weasel!" As an added attention getter, Cal reached out to grab a handful of Ivan's shirt.

"What have you done with Faith? Because I happen to know you're not on her list of favorite people. So why don't you tell me what you're doing in her apartment while she's in the shower? Did you follow her here? Is that it?"

"Is not it," Ivan sputtered.

"You better start talking," Cal warned him. "My patience is just about worn out."

"What is happening?" Natasha demanded as she rushed into the living room, tightening the belt on a red satin robe she was wearing.

Cal stared at her in surprise, while still maintaining his hold on Ivan. "What are you doing here?"

"Let Ivan go," Natasha cried.

"What's going on here? Are you and Ivan in on this together?"

The flash of fear in Natasha's eyes clinched it for Cal. "I knew it. Something *is* going on here. What have you done with Faith?" Using both hands, Cal yanked Ivan up to his eye level so that he could glare at him. "If you've so much as touched a hair on her head..."

"She invited us," Natasha declared.

"Like hell she did," Cal retorted.

"Is truth!" Ivan gasped, his toes dangling an inch above the floor.

"You wouldn't know the truth if it bit you," Cal snarled.

"Cal!" Faith stared at him in horror, pushing her glasses more firmly into place as if doubting what she was seeing. She certainly never expected this kind of scenario upon getting out of her shower. Hearing voices, she'd gotten dressed as quickly as possible, tugging on a white T-shirt and a navy rayon jumper. "What are you doing? Put Ivan down this instant. You're going to put his back out again."

Cal looked at Faith in disbelief. "Excuse me?"

"I said put him down."

Cal did. Reluctantly. But he didn't let Ivan go

"Why don't you tell me what's going on here?" he said to Faith with a calmness that was deceiving.

Faith recognized the fact that Cal was furious. He only used that tone of voice when he was seething. Keeping that in mind, she began searching for the right words, the best way of presenting the situation without setting Cal off again. Looking down, she realized her feet were still bare and that her toes were curling into the carpet like a nervous schoolgirl's.

Cal, also noticing her bare feet, once again tightened his hold on Ivan. "Somebody better tell me *right now* what the hell is going on here," he stated very, very softly.

"Is all mistake," Ivan gasped.

"Oh, for heaven's sake, Cal, let him go," Faith said in exasperation, her earlier nervousness forgotten. "I can't believe you were roughing him up that way in the first place."

Cal released Ivan with a muttered curse before turning to glare at Faith. "He answers the damn door half-undressed, looking like I just dragged him out of bed, and then he tells me you're in the shower. What the hell do you expect me to do?"

"You don't mean to tell me you thought that Ivan and I . . . ?"

"I didn't know what to think," Cal retorted, shifting uncomfortably.

"I can assure you that there's nothing sexual going on here," Faith said.

"Then why does Ivan have lipstick on his collar?" Cal demanded.

Faith sighed. "It's kind of a long story."

"I'm not going anywhere until I hear it," Cal stated, sitting down and making himself at home on her sofa. Then he gave her one of those looks—the stubborn kind, the kind that said she'd have to put a stick of dynamite under him to get him to budge.

"Ivan and Natasha have gotten themselves into a bit of trouble and I'm helping them out, that's all," Faith said.

"What kind of trouble?" Cal asked suspiciously.

"Smuggling trouble," Faith mumbled.

Cal frowned, certain he couldn't have heard her correctly. "What did you say?"

"Smuggling trouble," she repeated.

"Drugs?"

"Absolutely not!"

"What then?" he demanded.

"Diamonds."

"You better start at the beginning."

"It started with the tote bag. You remember, the one that wasn't mine?"

Cal nodded to indicate he was with her so far.

"You remember how you made me knock it over?" Seeing his frown, she added, "You picked up some of the things. The nightie..."

"Ah, that see-through number."

"I thought that might trigger your memory," she said tartly. "It was Natasha's."

"Really?"

Faith didn't appreciate his speculative look one bit, and was sure he was only using it to aggravate her. The glare she gave him warned him that she was angry enough to spit nails—right into his thick hide, if necessary.

Cal smiled. Faith was jealous. Good. Now she'd know how he felt that split instant when the door had opened and he'd found another man in her apartment.

"Apparently, we didn't pick everything up that had fallen out of the bag," Faith explained.

"I tried to search cabin while you were gone," Ivan stated. "But back injury prevented me from doing good job. Could not bend down. You have nice computer, by the way."

"I know," Cal retorted dryly. This was running like an Abbot and Costello movie.

"Ivan and Natasha stashed the stolen diamonds in a jar of face cream—" Faith told him.

"Face cream?" Cal interrupted.

"Was not my idea," Ivan inserted. "Was Natasha's idea."

"So that explains the infamous face-cream incident on board the ship," Cal murmured.

Faith nodded. "Ivan and Natasha broke into all the cabins on our level and stole all the face-cream jars."

"We did not know then who had bag," Ivan explained.

"And when they found out, they tried various means of recovering their property," Faith added.

"What kinds of various means?" Cal asked suspiciously.

"That's not important right now," Faith said, having decided the less Cal knew about that aspect of things the better. "You remember that jar of face cream you found this morning next to the bedside table? It turns out that that's the missing jar with the diamonds in it."

"Do not forget to include curse," Natasha reminded her.

"Curse?" Cal repeated.

Natasha nodded. "Diamonds of Midnight Ice have curse on them."

"Great," Cal muttered.

"I did not believe at first, either," Ivan said. "Was determined to find diamonds and keep. But now...now I believe. General sending henchmen after us made believer out of me."

This news did not please Cal, who growled, "What general and what henchmen?"

"When we docked in Vancouver, there were some men waiting for Natasha and Ivan," Faith replied.

"They were not friendly men. Were sent by general. General was dictator on Nabassi Island where Natasha and I worked," Ivan explained. "He was overthrown."

"After thirty years of power," Natasha inserted. "You must understand...nothing ever happens on Nabassi. That is why we were sent there. Was curse, of course."

"That you were sent there?" Cal asked in confusion.

"No, that general was overthrown. Only happened after he got Midnight Ice diamonds."

"So how did you two end up with them?" Cal demanded.

"When general was overthrown, island was in mess. We were visiting palace for diplomatic luncheon ... diamonds ended up in our lap," Ivan said.

"So did everything on table," Natasha added. "There was fight, you see ..."

"He does not need details. We ended up with diamonds and we took," Ivan stated.

"Was to be pension plan for us. Communist party in our country is no longer taking care of us," Natasha explained.

"Thirty years I devoted to mother country," Ivan exclaimed dramatically.

Cal was not impressed. "Yeah, right. So you grabbed the diamonds and ran? I'm assuming this deposed general has now sent a few of his henchmen after you to get his diamonds back."

Ivan nodded.

"Great," Cal muttered. "That's just great."

"Ivan and Natasha now regret what they did and they want to make amends," Faith added on their behalf.

"I can't believe you were so reckless as to get involved with this!" Cal exclaimed.

"I've checked into it," Faith said in her own defence. "Did a little research via some databanks I accessed from my computer here at the apartment. Their story checks out. There was a coup on Nabassi Island. I also found out that this dictator stole the diamonds from someone else, who stole them from someone else and so on."

"So what are you saying? That they should keep them?" Cal demanded.

"No. They should get rid of the diamonds. They've brought them nothing but trouble. I've already convinced Ivan and Natasha that the best thing to do would be to anonymously donate the diamonds to a worthy charity. If they do so, I've promised to help them in their honest attempts to start a new life here in America.''

"Well, you've got one thing right. The sooner we dump the diamonds the better. But why not just turn them over to the authorities?''

"There would be too many questions to answer," Faith replied. "And they'd deport Ivan and Natasha."

"Would serve them right," Cal muttered.

"He doesn't really mean that," Faith assured a nervous Ivan and Natasha.

"So you're just going to drop off a bag of diamonds at some charity?" Cal demanded.

Faith nodded. "Ivan and Natasha already selected the cause they'd like to support with their donation. Homelessness.''

"Because we could end up living in cardboard box and need assistance," Ivan said.

"There's a mission in the center of the city that is doing a lot of good work with the homeless," Cal noted. "If you're going to do this, we better get it over with quickly. Where are the diamonds now?''

"I have them," Faith said.

"Fine. Give them to me and I'll drop them off at the mission.''

"Actually, it was agreed that we'd all go together," Faith told him. "That was part of our agreement.''

"And what about the general's goons?''

"There's no way they could trace Ivan and Natasha to me. They were in disguise when we left the customs hall.''

Cal vaguely remembered the two strangers Faith had walked off with. "Let's get a move on, then. The sooner this is over with, the better. And you better put a note in with the diamonds explaining that these are the real thing and not paste.''

"We already did that," Faith said as she slipped into a pair of navy flats sitting by the front door.

"Let's go then."

"I must get dressed," Natasha said.

"You've got three minutes," Cal stated. To Faith, he said, "You never did say how Ivan got that lipstick on his collar."

"It was part of his disguise. He was dressed in heels and Natasha's trench coat. And he shaved his mustache, didn't you notice?"

"I had other things on my mind," Cal retorted. Like how he was going to get a chance to talk to Faith without an audience. "As soon as this little fiasco is settled, you and I have to talk," Cal informed Faith in no uncertain terms.

"There's nothing to talk about," Faith replied. As long as she and Cal were focused on Ivan and Natasha's problems, Faith was able to cope. In fact, in a way she almost welcomed this diversion. It had prevented her from dwelling on the pain Cal had caused her. She had no intention of rehashing things with Cal. "We have nothing to talk about," she repeated.

"Fine. Then you can just listen," Cal said. "Because this isn't finished between us."

"It's over," Faith said, refusing to look at him.

"The hell it is," Cal snapped.

"Am dressed now," Natasha stated as she rejoined them.

"The second this fiasco is over, we talk," Cal told Faith, his look one of implacable determination. "You've got my word on it."

The mission Cal had suggested was in the seedier part of the city, naturally enough, since that's where the need was the greatest. Ivan kissed the padded envelope containing the diamonds, saying his farewells in his own language as he passed the donation to the matronly woman seated in the mission's office. Natasha patted him on the shoulder consolingly.

Once they stepped outside the building, Natasha heaved a sigh of relief and said, "Curse will be over with now."

"Afraid not." Faith heard the words before she saw who spoke them. It was one of the bruisers she'd seen at the customs hall in Vancouver! This time, she had a feeling that the object that was being stuck into her side felt like a gun because it *was* a gun, and not a tube of lipstick as Natasha had pulled earlier. The man was accompanied by two others, who had pulled guns on Cal as well as on Ivan and Natasha. Guns with deadly-looking silencers.

"Look, this has nothing to do with Faith," Cal said. "Let her go."

"Shut up," the short stocky henchman holding the gun on him said. "And get moving. All of you."

Faith looked around, but there was no one on the street to help them as they were taken around the corner and shoved into an abandoned warehouse. "Where are the diamonds?" the stocky gunman growled.

"W-we no l-longer have M-midnight Ice d-diamonds," Ivan stuttered. "Gave them away to charity. Cannot get back."

The mercenary who seemed to be in charge made a tsk-tsk sound as he slowly shook his head. "That's too bad. The general *won't* be pleased."

"Tell general we are sorry we mistakenly took diamonds."

"That won't cut it with the general. No one steals from him and gets away with it. We need to teach you a lesson so it doesn't happen again."

On the verge of tears, Ivan assured them, "Will never happen again."

Cal tried reasoning with the men. "Look, the diamonds are gone. Killing us won't accomplish anything."

"It'll please the general and that's what we're paid to do," the leader said.

"Faith had nothing to do with this," Cal repeated. "Let her go."

"Sorry, pal, no can do. She's seen our faces. Can't leave a loose end like that lying around."

Desperate, Cal tried stalling for time. "How did you find us?"

"We followed you from the woman's apartment."

"And how did you know that's where Natasha and Ivan were?"

"We're professionals. We questioned people at the customs hall in Vancouver and found out that a woman in a babushka and trench coat left the *men's* room. Someone else remembered them getting into a compact car. Gave us a real accurate description, license plate and everything. It was a piece of cake after that. But enough of this small talk. It's time to take care of business." He lifted his gun.

Cal's eyes met Faith's. This was it. He mouthed the words *I love you* to her.

Faith's eyes widened. She heard a ringing in her ears. No, it wasn't ringing. It was . . . a beeper?

"Damn! I don't believe this," the leader muttered, looking down at the number displayed on his beeper. "It's the general. I've gotta answer. Sorry about this, folks. This will only take a minute. Watch them," he said curtly to the other two men.

Two of the hired henchmen kept Cal, Faith, Ivan and Natasha at gunpoint while their leader reached into his pocket, pulled out a portable cellular flip-phone and made a call.

Faith noted somewhat hysterically that he was using the phone as if making your run-of-the-mill business call. He spoke loudly enough that she was able to hear his side of the conversation. In fact, he was practically shouting. "What? That can't be! Right now? But we're not done here. . . . Okay, okay." He flipped the phone shut.

"What is it?" the short henchman asked.

"Forget this. We've got to go. Our man, the general, is back in power and wants us back in Nabassi immediately. He said to forget this project. He's got bigger fish to fry. The plane is waiting for us."

"What about them?" The short henchman pointed his gun at Faith, Cal, Ivan and Natasha as a group. "Shouldn't we tie 'em up, or something?"

"That'd take too long. We'll be long gone by the time they find help in this neighborhood."

Like the professionals they were, they disappeared as suddenly as they'd appeared. One moment the gunmen stood by the door with their guns trained on Cal and company, the next moment they were gone.

Just as quickly, Cal took Faith in his arms, holding her as if he'd never let her go. Faith closed her eyes and hung on to him for dear life, turning her head so that her cheek rested against his chest. She could hear his heart pounding, felt him curve his hand around the back of her neck, his fingertips brushing the skin just behind her ear. "It's all right," he kept whispering over and over again. "It's all over now. You're safe."

"Is lucky they left when they did," Ivan inserted. "One minute longer and I would have beaten them to pulp. Am expert in self-defense methods," he bragged, despite the fact that he'd been blatantly shivering in his boots only seconds before.

"Can it," Cal curtly ordered Ivan, glaring at him over Faith's bent head. "I think you've caused enough trouble for one day. Come on—" he curved one arm around Faith's shoulders "—let's get out of here before anything else goes wrong."

No one said anything during the ride back to Faith's apartment. Once they were inside, Faith kicked off her shoes and headed toward the kitchen.

Cal stopped her by placing his hand on her arm. "Where do you think you're going?"

"I thought I'd make us some tea, to calm our nerves."

"After we talk." Looking over at Ivan and Natasha listening in, Cal said, "Beat it."

"Is Michael Jackson song, yes?" Ivan said. "We are playing musical charades now?"

"No. You two are going to take a hike." Realizing that could be misunderstood, too, Cal said, "Faith and I have something private to discuss."

"They want to be alone," Natasha said, sounding eerily like Greta Garbo. "We will wait in guest room. Come, Ivan."

There was an awkward moment of silence that Faith was the first to break. "Look, I realize that people say things in emotional moments and they don't necessarily mean them.... I won't hold you to it, okay? So you can relax."

"You think I was lying when I said I love you?"

"You didn't actually say it. You mouthed the words. And no, I'm sure you do love me in your own way."

"What the hell is that supposed to mean?"

"As a friend," she translated.

"Sure I love you as a friend."

Faith's heart sank.

"I also love you the way a man loves the one woman on the face of the earth that's meant for him alone. For me, that woman is you, Faith."

She was stunned. She couldn't speak, could hardly breathe for the joy racing through her. Cal had actually said he loved her. She could barely believe it.

"Now, I realize that in the past, I haven't been a great advocate of matrimony," he went on to admit, "but some things have happened lately to make me reevaluate that position. I may have been blind and it may have taken me a while to get my act together, but I do see things clearly now. I see *you*, I love you and I'm not going to lose you now."

"But I thought you were afraid of commitment. Of marriage."

"Death is something to be afraid of," he retorted. "Mercenaries holding a gun on the woman I love—that's something to be afraid of. Not marriage. Not anymore."

Faith felt she had to voice her concern. "Maybe what you're feeling is just an aftereffect of the bigger-than-life experiences we've gone through this past week," she cautioned him. "I mean, think about it. We've had a romantic shipboard liaison followed by a brush with death. Not exactly your normal courtship."

"So what? There's nothing normal about the way I feel about you." Reaching out, he trailed his fingertips down the curve of her cheek. "It's exceptional, extraordinary and very, very rare. It's also very real. Hell, for all I know, I started falling in love with you ten years ago when you kissed me that New Year's Eve. I was just too scared to admit it or explore it. I'm not scared anymore, Faith. How about you? I can't read your mind. I need to know how you feel."

"I *know* I started falling in love with you ten years ago. I tried to get over you... it didn't work. I still love you and always will."

"Then marry me."

She hesitated. "I don't know..."

"I do. Marry me." He smiled his outlaw smile at her. "I'll hound you until you do."

"You're too accustomed to getting your own way, Masters. You know that?"

"You could work on reforming me," he suggested, his expression a challenging one.

"And where would *you* be working?" she retorted. "In the middle of some war-torn country reporting for your magazine?"

Cal shook his head. "The university where I taught last quarter has offered me a full-time teaching position starting in the fall. I've decided to accept it. Can you believe that? Me? A professor? I'm not sure how well a renegade like me will fit into that ivory-tower environment. I do like shaking up the status quo, though."

"I had noticed that about you," Faith murmured dryly.

"So what do you say? Will you marry me? Come on, Faith, don't keep me on pins and needles here."

"I'd have to be crazy to marry a man like you," she murmured reflectively. "You're stubborn, independent and difficult, not to mention too confident for your own good."

He scowled at her.

"On the other hand," she continued softly, "you're also caring, generous and protective, and I'd have to be crazy to let you get away. So, yes, I will marry you."

His smile was typically triumphant and very male. "Good. I didn't want to have to seduce you into saying yes...."

"I've got news for you, Cal. You can't seduce me into doing anything," she loftily informed him. "Although you're welcome to give it a try," she added with a look of wicked innocence.

An instant later, he was kissing her, claiming her as his, displaying his love for her. Faith looped her arms around his neck, reveling in the newfound richness of their embrace. For it held the confidence of declared love and commitment as well as the acknowledgement of life's frailty.

One kiss blended into the next until their happiness had to be expressed with breathless laughter and skimming kisses.

Cal was in such a good mood that even Ivan and Natasha's reappearance didn't upset him. "Congratulate us," Cal announced with a proud grin. "We're getting married."

"So are we," Ivan stated with his arm around Natasha. "Maybe could be double wedding? Do not need to decide now. See, I brought out bottle of general's champagne for us to be celebrating. We took from diplomatic luncheon last day on Nabassi. Champagne is vintage year."

"It certainly is!" Faith exclaimed, recognizing the year and the label. "Ivan, this bottle is worth several thousand dollars. Don't open it!"

"Do not be joking with me," Ivan replied.

"It's true," she assured him. "The magazine did an article on vintage champagnes in our current issue. Trust me, Ivan. This bottle is very valuable."

"Looks like we will not be homeless and living in cardboard box, after all," Natasha noted with a smile.

"It looks like we *all* have something to celebrate," Faith replied. "I've got some Asti Spumante in the fridge. We'll use that for our toast, instead." Faith quickly gathered the chilled bottle and some glasses from the kitchen. Once everyone had their tapered glass filled with bubbly, Ivan said, "To end of curse!"

"And to new beginnings," Cal added, his eyes on Faith in a look that told her how he felt more eloquently than mere words ever could.

"To new beginnings," Faith repeated softly. "For the two of us."

Together, Cal and Faith sealed that promise with a kiss, one that was as sweetly flavored as the sparkling wine and as passionately timeless as the love they shared.

* * * * *

Available in September from Silhouette Romance...

ONE OF A KIND MARRIAGE
by
Cathie Linz

It seemed like the perfect arrangement. Rafe Murphy could lose his little girl in a custody battle, and he needed a wife—fast. Jenny Benjamin's business was about to fail, and the only way to get to her trust fund was to get a husband. They were two people who believed a marriage of convenience would solve all of their problems. Yet this one-of-a-kind union was about to open up a whole new world of unexpected surprises....and unbridled passions!

Don't miss this delightful story. It's just a part of Silhouette Romance's special month of HASTY WEDDINGS—coming your way this September.

Take 4 bestselling love stories FREE

Plus get a FREE surprise gift!

SILHOUETTE® Desire®

JOAN JOHNSTON'S

SERIES CONTINUES!

Available in March, *The Cowboy Takes a Wife* (D #842) is the latest addition to Joan Johnston's sexy series about the lives and loves of the irresistible Whitelaw family. Set on a Wyoming ranch, this heart-wrenching story tells the tale of a single mother who desperately needs a husband—a very *big* husband—fast!

Don't miss *The Cowboy Takes a Wife* by Joan Johnston, only from Silhouette Desire.

MYSTERY WIFE
Annette Broadrick

She awoke in a French hospital—and found
handsome Raoul DuBois, claiming she was his wife,
Sherye, mother of their two children. But she didn't
recognize him or remember her identity. Whoever she
was, Sherye grew more attached to the children every
day—and the growing passion between her and
Raoul was like nothing they'd ever known before....

She's friend, wife, mother—she's you! And beside
each Special Woman stands a wonderfully *special*
man. It's a celebration of our heroines—and the men
who become part of their lives.

Don't miss **THAT SPECIAL WOMAN!** each month—
from some of your special authors! Only from
Silhouette Special Edition!

TSW494

SILHOUETTE *Desire*

COMING NEXT MONTH

#847 BEWITCHED—Jennifer Greene
Jock's Boys series
April's *Man of the Month*, Zach Connor, swore off family life long ago. But could he resist single mom Kirstin Grams and a matchmaking ghost who was intent on setting the two up?

#848 I'M GONNA GET YOU—Lass Small
Fabulous Brown Brothers
Tom Brown wanted Susan Lee McCrae, a honey-blond beauty with a streak of Texas stubbornness and a string of admirers. But he didn't want her just for now...he wanted her for always!

#849 MYSTERY LADY—Jackie Merritt
Saxon Brothers series
Sexy Rush Saxon was searching for riches, but found a floundering construction business and the last demure woman on earth. But Valentine LeClair held a secret she would never share with *this* ex-playboy.

#850 THE BRAINY BEAUTY—Suzanne Simms
Hazards, Inc. series
Egyptologist Samantha Wainwright had no time for an ex-Boy Scout doing a good deed. But for Jonathan Hazard, it wasn't just his job to protect this beauty...it was also his pleasure!

#851 RAFFERTY'S ANGEL—Caroline Cross
Years ago ex-agent Chase Rafferty had killed an innocent man. Now why was beautiful Maggie McKenna, the victim's wife, helping Chase get on with *his* life?

#852 STEALING SAVANNAH—Donna Carlisle
C.J. Cassidy needed to prove that he, was no longer a thief. But how could he when all he could think about was stealing Savannah Monterey's heart?

As seen on TV!
Free Gift Offer

With a Free Gift proof-of-purchase from any Silhouette® book,
you can receive a beautiful cubic zirconia pendant.

This gorgeous marquise-shaped stone is a genuine cubic
zirconia—accented by an 18" gold tone necklace.

(Approximate retail value $19.95)

Send for yours today...
compliments of ▼ *Silhouette*®
™

To receive your free gift, a cubic zirconia pendant, send us one original proof-of-purchase, photocopies not accepted, from the back of any Silhouette Romance™, Silhouette Desire®, Silhouette Special Edition®, Silhouette Intimate Moments® or Silhouette Shadows™ title for January, February or March 1994 at your favorite retail outlet, together with the Free Gift Certificate, plus a check or money order for $2.50 (do not send cash) to cover postage and handling, payable to Silhouette Free Gift Offer. We will send you the specified gift. Allow 6 to 8 weeks for delivery. Offer good until March 31st, 1994 or while quantities last. Offer valid in the U.S. and Canada only.

Free Gift Certificate

Name: _____

Address: _____

City: _____ State/Province: _____ Zip/Postal Code: _____

Mail this certificate, one proof-of-purchase and a check or money order for postage and handling to: SILHOUETTE FREE GIFT OFFER 1994. In the U.S.: 3010 Walden Avenue, P.O. Box 9057, Buffalo NY 14269-9057. In Canada: P.O. Box 622, Fort Erie, Ontario L2Z 5X3

FREE GIFT OFFER
ONE PROOF-OF-PURCHASE

079-KBZ

To collect your fabulous FREE GIFT, a cubic zirconia pendant, you must include this original proof-of-purchase for each gift with the properly completed Free Gift Certificate.

079-KBZ